Emmy wa...

thoughts, m...

That tiresome girl, he reflected. Why do I have this urge to do something to improve her life? For all I know she is perfectly content with the way she lives. She is young; she could get a job wherever she wishes, buy herself some decent clothes, meet people, find a boyfriend. All of which was nonsense, and he knew it. She deserved better.

But even if she had a chance to change, he knew that she wouldn't leave her home.

The professor put down the notes he was studying, took off his spectacles, polished them and put them back onto his nose.

"This is ridiculous," he said to himself. "I don't even know the girl."

He forebore from adding that he knew Ermentrude as if she were himself, had done since he had first seen her.

SUPER ROMANCE

Romance readers around the world were sad to note the passing of **Betty Neels** in June 2001. Her career spanned thirty years, and she continued to write into her ninetieth year. To her millions of fans, Betty epitomized the romance writer, and yet she began writing almost by accident. She had retired from nursing, but her inquiring mind still sought stimulation. Her new career was born when she heard a lady in her local library bemoaning the lack of good romance novels. Betty's first book, *Sister Peters in Amsterdam*, was published in 1969, and she eventually completed 134 books. Her novels offer a reassuring warmth that was very much a part of her own personality. She was a wonderful writer, and she will be greatly missed. Her spirit and genuine talent will live on in all her stories.

THE BEST *of*

BETTY NEELS

The Mistletoe Kiss

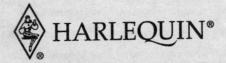

HARLEQUIN®

TORONTO • NEW YORK • LONDON
AMSTERDAM • PARIS • SYDNEY • HAMBURG
STOCKHOLM • ATHENS • TOKYO • MILAN • MADRID
PRAGUE • WARSAW • BUDAPEST • AUCKLAND

PLEASE RECYCLE • THIS PRODUCT IS RECYCLABLE •

Recycling programs
for this product may
not exist in your area.

ISBN-13: 978-0-373-19960-0

THE MISTLETOE KISS

CHAPTER ONE

IT WAS a blustery October evening, and the mean little wind was blowing old newspapers, tin cans and empty wrapping papers to and fro along the narrow, shabby streets of London's East End. It had blown these through the wide entrance to the massive old hospital towering over the rows of houses and shops around it, but its doors were shut against them, and inside the building it was quiet, very clean and tidy. In place of the wind there was warm air, carrying with it a whiff of disinfectant tinged with floor polish and the patients' suppers, something not experienced by those attending the splendid new hospitals now replacing the old ones. There they were welcomed by flowers, a café, signposts even the most foolish could read and follow...

St Luke's had none of these—two hundred years old and condemned to be closed, there was no point in wasting money. Besides, the people who frequented its dim corridors weren't there to look at flowers, they followed the painted pointed finger on its walls telling them to go to Casualty, X-Ray, the wards or Out Patients, and, when they got there, settled onto the wooden benches in the waiting rooms and had a good gossip with whoever was next to them. It was their hospital, they felt at home in it; its lengthy corridors held no worries for them, nor did the elderly lifts and endless staircases.

They held no worries for Ermentrude Foster, skimming up to the top floor of the hospital, intent on delivering the message which had been entrusted to her as quickly as possible before joining the throng of people queuing for buses on their way home. The message had nothing to do with her, actually; Professor ter Mennolt's secretary had come out of her office as Ermentrude had been getting into her outdoor things, her hours of duty at the hospital telephone switchboard finished for the day, and had asked her to run up to his office with some papers he needed.

'I'm late,' said the secretary urgently. 'And my boyfriend's waiting for me. We're going to see that new film…'

Ermentrude, with no prospect of a boyfriend or a film, obliged.

Professor ter Mennolt, spectacles perched on his magnificent nose, was immersed in the papers before him on his desk. A neurologist of some renown, he was at St Luke's by invitation, reading a paper on muscular dystrophies, lecturing students, lending his knowledge on the treatment of those patients suffering from diseases of the nervous system. Deep in the study of a case of myasthenia gravis, his, 'Come,' was absent-minded in answer to a knock on the door, and he didn't look up for a few moments.

Ermentrude, uncertain whether to go in or not, had poked her head round the door, and he studied it for a moment. A pleasant enough face, not pretty, but the nose was slightly tip-tilted, the eyes large and the wide mouth was smiling.

Ermentrude bore his scrutiny with composure, opened the door and crossed the room to his desk.

'Miss Crowther asked me to bring you this,' she told him cheerfully. 'She had a date and wanted to get home…'

The professor eyed her small, slightly plump person and looked again at her face, wondering what colour her hair was; a scarf covered the whole of it, and since she was wearing a plastic mac he deduced that it was raining.

'And you, Miss…?' He paused, his eyebrows raised.

'Foster, Ermentrude Foster.' She smiled at him. 'Almost as bad as yours, isn't it?' Undeterred by the cold blue eyes staring at her, she explained, 'Our names,' just in case he hadn't understood. 'Awkward, aren't they?'

He had put down his pen. 'You work here in the hospital?'

'Me? Yes, I'm a telephonist. Are you going to be here for a long time?'

'I can hardly see why the length of my stay should interest you, Miss Foster.'

'Well, no, it doesn't, really.' She gave him a kind smile. 'I thought you might be a bit lonely up here all by yourself. Besides I rather wanted to see you—I'd heard about you, of course.'

'Should I feel gratified at your interest?' he asked coldly.

'No, no, of course not. But they all said how handsome you were, and not a bit like a Dutchman.' She paused then, because his eyes weren't cold any more, they were like blue ice.

He said levelly, 'Miss Foster, I think it might be a good idea if you were to leave this room. I have work to do, and interruptions, especially such as yours, can be annoying. Be good enough to tell Miss Crowther on no account to send you here again.'

He bent over his work and didn't watch her go.

Ermentrude went slowly back through the hospital and out into the wet October evening to join the queue at the nearest bus stop, thinking about the professor. A handsome man, she conceded; fair hair going grey, a splendid nose, heavy-lidded eyes and a firm mouth—which was a bit thin, perhaps. Even sitting at his desk it was easy to see that he was a very large man. Still quite young, too. The hospital grapevine knew very little about him, though.

She glanced back over her shoulder; there were still lighted windows on the top floor of the hospital; one of them would be his. She sighed. He hadn't liked her and, of course, that was to be understood. She had been ticked off on several occasions for not being respectful enough with those senior to her—and they were many—but that hadn't cured her from wanting to be friends with everyone.

Born and brought up in a rural part of Somerset, where everyone knew everyone else, she had never quite got used to the Londoners' disregard for those around them. Oblivious of the impatient prod from the woman behind her, she thought of the professor sitting up there, so far from anyone… And he was a foreigner, too.

Professor ter Mennolt, unaware of her concern, adjusted his spectacles on his nose and addressed himself to the pile of work on his desk, perfectly content with his lot, careless of the fact that he was alone and a foreigner. He had quite forgotten Ermentrude.

The bus, by the time Ermentrude got onto it, was packed, and, since it was raining, the smell of wet raincoats was overpowering. She twitched her small nose and wondered what was for supper, and, after a ten-minute ride squashed between two stout women, got off with relief.

Five minutes' walk brought her to her home, midway down a terrace of small, neat houses in a vaguely shabby street, their front doors opening onto the pavement. She unlocked the door, calling, 'It's me,' as she did so, and opened a door in the narrow hallway. Her mother was there, sitting at a small table, knitting. Still knitting, she looked up and smiled.

'Emmy—hello, love. Supper's in the oven, but would you like a cup of tea first?'

'I'll make it, Mother. Was there a letter from Father?'

'Yes, dear, it's on the mantelpiece. Have you had a busy day?'

'So-so. I'll get the tea.'

Emmy took off her raincoat and scarf, hung them on a peg in the hall and went into the kitchen, a small, old-fashioned place with cheerful, cheap curtains and some rather nice china on the dresser shelves. About all there was left of her old home, thought Emmy, gathering cups and saucers and opening the cake tin.

Her father had taught at a large school in Somerset, and they had lived in a nearby village in a nice old house with a large garden and heavenly views. But he had been made redundant and been unable to find another post! Since an elderly aunt had recently died and left him this small house, and a colleague had told him of a post in London, they had come here to live. The post wasn't as well paid, and Mrs Foster found that living in London was quite a different matter from living in a small village with a garden which supplied her with vegetables all the year round and hens who laid fresh eggs each day.

Emmy, watching her mother coping with household bills, had given up her hopes of doing something artistic. She drew and painted and embroidered exquisitely, and had set her sights on attending a school of needlework and then starting up on her own—she wasn't sure as what.

There had been an advertisement in the paper for a switch-board operator at St Luke's, and she had gone along and got the job.

She had no experience of course, but she had a pleasant voice, a nice manner and she'd been keen to have work. She'd been given a week's training, a month's trial and then had been taken on permanently. It wasn't what she wanted to do, but the money was a great help, and one day her father would find a better post. Indeed, he was already well thought of and there was a chance of promotion.

She made the tea, offered a saucer of milk to Snoodles the cat, handed a biscuit to George the elderly dachshund, and carried the tray into the sitting room.

Over tea she read her father's letter. He had been standing in for a school inspector, and had been away from home for a week. He would be coming home for the weekend, he wrote, but he had been asked to continue covering for his colleague for the next month or so. If he accepted, then it would be possible for Mrs Foster to be with him when it was necessary for him to go further afield.

'Mother, that's wonderful—Father hates being away from home, but if you're with him he won't mind as much, and if they're pleased with him he'll get a better job.'

'I can't leave you here on your own.'

'Of course you can, Mother. I've Snoodles and George for company, and we know the neighbours well enough if I should need anything. I can come home for my lunch hour and take George for a quick walk. I'm sure Father will agree to that. Besides, Father gets moved from one school to the other, doesn't he? When he is nearer home you can be here.'

'I'm sure I don't know, love. The idea of you being on your own...'

Emmy refilled their cups. 'If I had a job in another

town, I'd be on my own in some bedsitter, wouldn't I? But I'm at home. And I'm twenty-three…'

'Well, I know your father would like me to be with him. We'll talk about it at the weekend.'

By breakfast time the next morning Mrs Foster was ready to concede that there was really no reason why she shouldn't join her husband, at least for short periods. 'For you're home by six o'clock most evenings, when it's still quite light, and I dare say we'll be home most weekends.'

Emmy agreed cheerfully. She was due to go on night duty in a week's time, but there was no need to remind her mother of that. She went off to catch a bus to the hospital, glad that the rain had ceased and it was a nice autumn day.

The switchboard was busy; it always was on Fridays. Last-minute plans for the weekend, she supposed, on the part of the hospital medical staff—people phoning home, making appointments to play golf, arranging to meet to discuss some case or other—and all these over and above the outside calls, anxious family wanting news of a patient, doctors' wives with urgent messages, other hospitals wanting to contact one or other of the consulting staff. It was almost time for her midday dinner when a woman's voice, speaking English with a strong accent, asked to speak to Professor ter Mennolt.

'Hold the line while I get him for you,' said Emmy. His wife, she supposed, and decided that she didn't much like the voice—very haughty. The voice became a person in her mind's eye, tall and slim and beautiful—because the professor wouldn't look at anything less—and well used to having her own way.

He wasn't in his room, and he wasn't on any of the wards she rang. She paused in her search to reassure the voice that she was still trying, and was rewarded by being told to be quick. He wasn't in Theatre, but he was in the Pathology Lab.

'There you are,' said Emmy, quite forgetting to add 'sir'. 'I've a call for you; will you take it there?'

'Only if it's urgent; I'm occupied at the moment.'

'It's a lady,' Emmy told him. 'She told me to hurry. She speaks English with an accent.'

'Put the call through here.' He sounded impatient.

It wouldn't hurt him to say thank you, reflected Emmy as she assured his caller that she was being put through at once. She got no thanks from her either. 'They must suit each other admirably,' said Emmy under her breath, aware that the bossy woman who went around with a clipboard was coming towards her. As usual she was full of questions—had there been delayed calls? Had Ermentrude connected callers immediately? Had she noted the times?

Emmy said yes to everything. She was a conscientious worker, and although it wasn't a job she would have chosen she realised that she was lucky to have it, and it wasn't boring. She was relieved for her dinner hour presently, and went along to the canteen to eat it in the company of the ward clerks and typists. She got on well with them, and they for their part liked her, though considering her hopelessly out of date, and pitying her in a friendly way because she had been born and brought up in the country and had lacked the pleasures of London. She lacked boyfriends, too, despite their efforts to get her to join them for a visit to a cinema or a pub.

They didn't hold it against her; she was always goodnatured, ready to help, willing to cover a relief telephonist if she had a date, listening to emotional outbursts about boyfriends with a sympathetic ear. They agreed among themselves that she was all right—never mind the posh voice; she couldn't help that, could she, with a father who was a schoolmaster? Besides, it sounded OK on the phone, and that was what her job was all about, wasn't it?

Home for the weekend, Mr Foster agreed with Emmy that there was no reason why she shouldn't be at home on her own for a while.

'I'll be at Coventry for a week or ten days, and then several schools in and around London. You don't mind, Emmy?'

She saw her mother and father off on Sunday evening, took George for a walk and went to bed. She wasn't a nervous girl and there were reassuringly familiar noises all around her: Mr Grant next door practising the flute, the teenager across the street playing his stereo, old Mrs Grimes, her other neighbour, shouting at her husband who was deaf. She slept soundly.

She was to go on night duty the next day, which meant that she would be relieved at dinner time and go back to work at eight o'clock that evening. Which gave her time in the afternoon to do some shopping at the row of small shops at the end of the street, take George for a good walk and sit down to a leisurely meal.

There was no phone in the house, so she didn't have to worry about her mother ringing up later in the evening. She cut sandwiches, put *Sense and Sensibility* and a much thumbed *Anthology of English Verse* in her shoulder bag with the sandwiches, and presently went back through the dark evening to catch her bus.

When she reached the hospital the noise and bustle of the day had subsided into subdued footsteps, the distant clang of the lifts and the occasional squeak of a trolley's wheels. The relief telephonist was waiting for her, an elderly woman who manned the switchboard between night and day duties.

'Nice and quiet so far,' she told Emmy. 'Hope you have a quiet night.'

Emmy settled herself in her chair, made sure that everything was as it should be and got out the knitting she had pushed in with the books at the last minute. She would knit until one of the night porters brought her coffee.

There were a number of calls: enquiries about patients, anxious voices asking advice as to whether they should bring a sick child to the hospital, calls to the medical staff on duty.

Later, when she had drunk her cooling coffee and picked up her neglected knitting once again, Professor ter Mennolt, on his way home, presumably, paused by her.

He eyed the knitting. 'A pleasant change from the daytime rush,' he remarked. 'And an opportunity to indulge your womanly skills.'

'Well, I don't know about that,' said Emmy sensibly. 'It keeps me awake in between calls! It's very late; oughtn't you to be in your bed?'

'My dear young lady, surely that is no concern of yours?'

'Oh, I'm not being nosey,' she assured him. 'But everyone needs a good night's sleep, especially people like you—people who use their brains a lot.'

'That is your opinion, Ermentrude? It is Ermentrude, isn't it?'

'Yes, and yes. At least, it's my father's opinion.'

'Your father is a medical man, perhaps?' he asked smoothly.

'No, a schoolmaster.'

'Indeed? Then why are you not following in his footsteps?'

'I'm not clever. Besides, I like sewing and embroidery.'

'And you are a switchboard operator.' His tone was dry.

'It's a nice, steady job,' said Emmy, and picked up her knitting. 'Goodnight, Professor ter Mennolt.'

'Goodnight, Ermentrude.' He had gone several paces when he turned on his heel. 'You have an old-fashioned name. I am put in mind of a demure young lady with ringlets and a crinoline, downcast eyes and a soft and gentle voice.'

She looked at him, her mouth half-open.

'You have a charming voice, but I do not consider you demure, nor do you cast down your eyes—indeed their gaze is excessively lively.'

He went away then, leaving her wondering what on earth he had been talking about.

'Of course, he's foreign,' reflected Emmy out loud. 'And besides that he's one of those clever people whose feet aren't quite on the ground, always bothering about people's insides.'

A muddled statement which nonetheless satisfied her.

Audrey, relieving her at eight o'clock the next morning, yawned widely and offered the information that she hated day duty, hated the hospital, hated having to work. 'Lucky you,' she observed. 'All day to do nothing…'

'I shall go to bed,' said Emmy mildly, and took herself off home.

It was a slow business, with the buses crammed with people going to work, and then she had to stop at the shops at the end of the street and buy bread, eggs, bacon, food for Snoodles and more food for George. Once home, with the door firmly shut behind her, she put on the kettle, fed the animals and let George into the garden. Snoodles tailed him, warned not to go far.

She had her breakfast, tidied up, undressed and had a shower and, with George and Snoodles safely indoors, went to her bed. The teenager across the street hadn't made a sound so far; hopefully he had a job or had gone off with his pals. If Mr Grant and Mrs Grimes kept quiet, she would have a good sleep... She had barely had time to form the thought before her eyes shut.

It was two o'clock when she was woken by a hideous mixture of sound: Mr Grant's flute—played, from the sound of it, at an open window—Mrs Grimes bellowing at her husband in the background and, almost drowning these, the teenager enjoying a musical session.

Emmy turned over and buried her head in the pillow, but it was no use; she was wide awake now and likely to stay so. She got up and showered and dressed, had a cup of tea and a sandwich, made sure that Snoodles was asleep, put a lead on George's collar and left the house.

She had several hours of leisure still; she boarded an almost empty bus and sat with George on her lap as it bore them away from Stepney, along Holborn and into the Marylebone Road. She got off here and crossed the street to Regent's Park.

It was pleasant here, green and open with the strong scent of autumn in the air. Emmy walked briskly, with George trotting beside her.

'We'll come out each day,' she promised him. 'A pity the parks are all so far away, but a bus ride's nice enough, isn't it? And you shall have a good tea when we get home.'

The afternoon was sliding into dusk as they went back home. George gobbled his tea and curled up on his chair in the kitchen while Snoodles went out. Mrs Grimes had stopped shouting, but Mr Grant was still playing the flute, rivalling the din from across the street. Emmy ate her tea, stuffed things into her bag and went to work.

* * *

Audrey had had a busy day and was peevish. 'I spent the whole of my two hours off looking for some decent tights—the shops around here are useless.'

'There's that shop in Commercial Road…' began Emmy.

'There?' Audrey was scornful. 'I wouldn't be seen dead in anything from there.' She took a last look at her face, added more lipstick and patted her blonde head. 'I'm going out this evening. So long.'

Until almost midnight Emmy was kept busy. From time to time someone passing through from the entrance hall stopped for a word, and one of the porters brought her coffee around eleven o'clock with the news that there had been a pile-up down at the docks and the accident room was up to its eyes.

'They phoned,' said Emmy, 'but didn't say how bad it was—not to me, that is. I switched them straight through. I hope they're not too bad.'

'Couple of boys, an old lady, the drivers—one of them's had a stroke.'

Soon she was busy again, with families phoning with anxious enquiries. She was eating her sandwiches in the early hours of the morning when Professor ter Mennolt's voice, close to her ear, made her jump.

'I am relieved to see that you are awake and alert, Ermentrude.'

She said, round the sandwich. 'Well, of course I am. That's not a nice thing to say, sir.'

'What were you doing in a bus on the Marylebone Road when you should have been in bed asleep, recruiting strength for the night's work?'

'I was going to Regent's Park with George. He had a good walk.' She added crossly, 'And *you* should try to sleep with someone playing the flute on one side of the house, Mrs Grimes shouting on the other and that wretched boy with his stereo across the street.'

The professor was leaning against the wall, his hands in the pockets of his beautifully tailored jacket. 'I have misjudged you, Ermentrude. I am sorry. Ear plugs, perhaps?' And, when she shook her head, 'Could you not beg a bed from a friend? Or your mother have a word with the neighbours?'

'Mother's with Father,' said Emmy, and took a bite of sandwich. 'I can't leave the house because of George and Snoodles.'

'George?'

'Our dog, and Snoodles is the cat.'

'So you are alone in the house?' He stared down at her. 'You are not nervous?'

'No, sir.'

'You live close by?'

What a man for asking questions, thought Emmy, and wished he didn't stare so. She stared back and said 'Yes,' and wished that he would go away; she found him unsettling. She remembered something. 'I didn't see you on the bus...'

He smiled. 'I was in the car, waiting for the traffic lights.'

She turned to the switchboard, then, and put through two calls, and he watched her. She had pretty hands, nicely well-cared for, and though her hair was mouse-brown there seemed to be a great deal of it, piled neatly in a coil at the back of her head. Not in the least pretty, but with eyes like hers that didn't matter.

He bade her goodnight, and went out to his car and forgot her, driving to his charming little house in Chelsea where Beaker, who ran it for him, would have left coffee and sandwiches for him in his study, his desk light on and a discreet lamp burning in the hall.

* * *

Although it was almost two o'clock he sat down to go through his letters and messages while he drank the coffee, hot and fragrant in the Thermos. There was a note, too, written in Beaker's spidery hand: Juffrouw Anneliese van Moule had phoned at eight o'clock and again at ten. The professor frowned and glanced over to the answering machine. It showed the red light, and he went and switched it on.

In a moment a petulant voice, speaking in Dutch, wanted to know where he was. 'Surely you should be home by ten o'clock in the evening. I asked you specially to be home, did I not? Well, I suppose I must forgive you and give you good news. I am coming to London in three days' time—Friday. I shall stay at Brown's Hotel, since you are unlikely to be home for most of the day, but I expect to be taken out in the evenings—and there will be time for us to discuss the future.

'I wish to see your house; I think it will not do for us when we are married, for I shall live with you in London when you are working there, but I hope you will give up your work in England and live at Huis ter Mennolt—'

The professor switched off. Anneliese's voice had sounded loud as well as peevish, and she was reiterating an argument they had had on several occasions. He had no intention of leaving his house; it was large enough. He had some friends to dine, but his entertaining was for those whom he knew well. Anneliese would wish to entertain on a grand scale, fill the house with acquaintances; he would return home each evening to a drawing room full of people he neither knew nor wished to know.

He reminded himself that she would be a most suitable wife; in Holland they had a similar circle of friends and acquaintances, and they liked the same things—the theatre, concerts, art exhibitions—and she was ambitious.

At first he had been amused and rather touched by that,

until he had realised that her ambition wasn't for his success in his profession but for a place in London society. She already had that in Holland, and she had been careful never to admit to him that that was her goal… He reminded himself that she was the woman he had chosen to marry and once she had understood that he had no intention of altering his way of life when they were married she would understand how he felt.

After all, when they were in Holland she could have all the social life she wanted; Huis ter Mennolt was vast, and there were servants enough and lovely gardens. While he was working she could entertain as many of her friends as she liked—give dinner parties if she wished, since the house was large enough to do that with ease. Here at the Chelsea house, though, with only Beaker and a daily woman to run the place, entertaining on such a scale would be out of the question. The house, roomy though it was, was too small.

He went to bed then, and, since he had a list the following day, he had no time to think about anything but his work.

He left the hospital soon after ten o'clock the next evening. Ermentrude was at her switchboard, her back towards him. He gave her a brief glance as he passed.

Anneliese had phoned again, Beaker informed him, but would leave no message. 'And, since I needed some groceries, I switched on the answering machine, sir,' he said, 'since Mrs Thrupp, splendid cleaner though she is, is hardly up to answering the telephone.'

The professor went to his study and switched on the machine, and stood listening to Anneliese. Her voice was no longer petulant, but it was still loud. 'My plane gets in at half past ten on Friday—Heathrow,' she told him. 'I'll look out for you. Don't keep me waiting, will you, Ruerd?

Shall we dine at Brown's? I shall be too tired to talk much, and I'll stay for several days, anyway.'

He went to look at his appointments book on his desk. He would be free to meet her, although he would have to go back to his consulting rooms for a couple of hours before joining her at Brown's Hotel.

He sat down at his desk, took his glasses from his breast pocket, put them on and picked up the pile of letters before him. He was aware that there was a lack of lover-like anticipation at the thought of seeing Anneliese. Probably because he hadn't seen her for some weeks. Moreover, he had been absorbed in his patients. In about a month's time he would be going back to Holland for a month or more; he would make a point of seeing as much of Anneliese as possible.

He ate his solitary dinner, and went back to his study to write a paper on spina bifida, an exercise which kept him engrossed until well after midnight.

Past the middle of the week already, thought Emmy with satisfaction, getting ready for bed the next morning—three more nights and she would have two days off. Her mother would be home too, until she rejoined her father later in the week, and then he would be working in and around London. Emmy heaved a tired, satisfied sigh and went to sleep until, inevitably, the strains of the flute woke her. It was no use lying there and hoping they would stop; she got up, had a cup of tea and took George for a walk.

It was raining when she went to work that evening, and she had to wait for a long time for a bus. The elderly relief telephonist was off sick, and Audrey was waiting for her when she got there, already dressed to leave, tapping her feet with impatience.

'I thought you'd never get here…'

'It's still only two minutes to eight,' said Emmy mildly. 'Is there anything I should know?'

She was taking off her mac and headscarf as she spoke, and when Audrey said no, there wasn't, Emmy sat down before the switchboard, suddenly hating the sight of it. The night stretched ahead of her, endless hours of staying alert. The thought of the countless days and nights ahead in the years to come wasn't to be borne.

She adjusted her headpiece and arranged everything just so, promising herself that she would find another job, something where she could be out of doors for at least part of the day. And meet people…a man who would fall in love with her and want to marry her. A house in the country, mused Emmy, dogs and cats and chickens and children, of course…

She was roused from this pleasant dream by an outside call, followed by more of them; it was always at this time of the evening that people phoned to make enquiries.

She was kept busy throughout the night. By six o'clock she was tired, thankful that in another couple of hours she would be free. Only three more nights; she thought sleepily of what she would do. Window shopping with her mother? And if the weather was good enough they could take a bus to Hampstead Heath…

A great blast of sound sent her upright in her chair, followed almost at once by a call from the police—there had been a bomb close to Fenchurch Street Station. Too soon to know how many were injured, but they would be coming to St Luke's!

Emmy, very wide awake now, began notifying everyone—the accident room, the house doctors' rooms, the wards, X-Ray, the path lab. And within minutes she was kept busy, ringing the consultants on call, theatre staff, technicians, ward sisters on day duty. She had called the professor, but hadn't spared him a thought, nor had she seen him as he came to the hospital, for there was a great deal of orderly coming and going as the ambulances began to arrive.

She had been busy; now she was even more so. Anxious relatives were making frantic calls, wanting to know where the injured were and how they were doing. But it was too soon to know anything. The accident room was crowded; names were sent to her as they were given, but beyond letting callers know that they had that particular person in the hospital there was no more information to pass on.

Emmy went on answering yet more calls, putting through outside calls too—to other hospitals, the police, someone from a foreign embassy who had heard that one of the staff had been injured. She answered them all in her quiet voice, trying to ignore a threatening headache.

It seemed a very long time before order emerged from the controlled chaos. There were no more ambulances now, and patients who needed admission were being taken to the wards. The accident room, still busy, was dealing with the lesser injured; the hospital was returning to its normal day's work.

It was now ten o'clock. Emmy, looking at her watch for the first time in hours, blinked. Where was Audrey? Most of the receptionists had come in, for they had rung to tell her so, but not Audrey. Emmy was aware that she was hungry, thirsty and very tired, and wondered what to do about it. She would have to let someone know…

Audrey tapped on her shoulder. She said airily, 'Sorry I'm late. I didn't fancy coming sooner; I bet the place was a shambles. I knew you wouldn't mind…'

'I do mind, though,' said Emmy. 'I mind very much. I've had a busy time, and I should have been off duty two hours ago.'

'Well, you were here, weren't you? Did you expect me

to come tearing in in the middle of all the fuss just so's you could go off duty? Besides, you're not doing anything; you only go to bed…'

The professor, on his way home, paused to listen to this with interest. Ermentrude, he could see, was looking very much the worse for wear; she had undoubtedly had a busy time of it, and she had been up all night, whereas the rest of them had merely got out of their beds earlier than usual.

He said now pleasantly, 'Put on your coat, Ermentrude; I'll drive you home. We can take up the matter of the extra hours you have worked later on. Leave it to me.'

Emmy goggled at him, but he gave her no chance to speak. He said, still pleasantly, to Audrey, 'I'm sure you have a good reason for not coming on duty at the usual time.' He smiled thinly. 'It will have to be a good one, will it not?'

He swept Emmy along, away from a pale Audrey, out of the doors and into his Bentley. 'Tell me where you live,' he commanded.

'There is no need to take me home, I'm quite able—'

'Don't waste my time. We're both tired, and I for one am feeling short-tempered.'

'So am I,' snapped Emmy. 'I want a cup of tea, and I'm hungry.'

'That makes two of us. Now, where do you live, Ermentrude?'

CHAPTER TWO

EMMY told him her address in a cross voice, sitting silently until he stopped before her home. She said gruffly, 'Thank you, Professor. Good morning,' and made to open her door. He shook her hand and released it, and she put it in her lap. Then he got out, opened the door, crossed the pavement with her, took the key from her and opened the house door. George rushed to meet them while Snoodles, a cat not to be easily disturbed, sat on the bottom step of the stairs, watching.

Emmy stood awkwardly in the doorway with George, who was making much of her. She said again, 'Thank you, Professor,' and peered up at his face.

'The least you can do is offer me a cup of tea,' he told her, and came into the hall, taking her with him and closing the door. 'You get that coat off and do whatever you usually do while I put on the kettle.'

He studied her face. Really, the girl was very plain; for a moment he regretted the impulse which had urged him to bring her home. She had been quite capable of getting herself there; he had formed the opinion after their first meeting that she was more than capable of dealing with any situation—and with a sharp tongue, too. She looked at him then, though, and he saw how tired she was. He said in a placid voice, 'I make a very good cup of tea.'

She smiled. 'Thank you. The kitchen's here.'

She opened a door and ushered him into the small room at the back of the house, which was, he saw, neat and very clean, with old-fashioned shelves and a small dresser. There was a gas stove against one wall—an elderly model, almost a museum piece, but still functioning, he was relieved to find.

Emmy went away and he found tea, milk and sugar while the kettle boiled, took mugs and a brown teapot from the dresser and set them on the table while Emmy fed Snoodles and George.

They drank their tea presently, sitting opposite each other saying little, and when the professor got to his feet Emmy made no effort to detain him. She thanked him again, saw him to the door and shut it the moment he had driven away, intent on getting to her bed as quickly as possible. She took a slice of bread and butter and a slab of cheese with her, and George and Snoodles, who had sidled upstairs with her, got onto the bed too—which was a comfort for she was feeling hard done by and put upon.

'It's all very well,' she told them peevishly. 'He'll go home to a doting wife—slippers in one hand and bacon and eggs in the other.'

She swallowed the last of the cheese and went to sleep, and not even the flute or Mrs Grimes' loud voice could wake her.

The professor got into his car, and as he drove away his bleep sounded. He was wanted back at St Luke's; one of the injured had developed signs of a blood clot on the brain. So instead of going home he went back and spent the next few hours doing everything in his power to keep his patient alive—something which proved successful, so that in the early afternoon he was at last able to go home.

He let himself into his house, put his bag down and trod into the sitting room, to come to a halt just inside the door.

'Anneliese—I forgot…'

She was a beautiful girl with thick fair hair cut short by an expert hand, perfect features and big blue eyes, and she was exquisitely made-up. She was dressed in the height of fashion and very expensively, too. She made a charming picture, marred by the ill-temper on her face.

She spoke in Dutch, not attempting to hide her bad temper.

'Really, Ruerd, what am I to suppose you mean by that? That man of yours, Beaker—who, by the way, I shall discharge as soon as we are married—refused to phone the hospital—said you would be too busy to answer. Since when has a consultant not been free to answer the telephone when he wishes?'

He examined several answers to that and discarded them. 'I am sorry, my dear. There was a bomb; it exploded close to St Luke's early this morning. It was necessary for me to be there—there were casualties. Beaker was quite right; I shouldn't have answered the phone.'

He crossed the room and bent to kiss her cheek. 'He is an excellent servant; I have no intention of discharging him.' He spoke lightly, but she gave him a questioning look. They had been engaged for some months now, and she was still not sure that she knew him. She wasn't sure if she loved him either, but he could offer her everything she wanted in life; they knew the same people and came from similar backgrounds. Their marriage would be entirely suitable.

She decided to change her tactics. 'I'm sorry for being cross. But I was disappointed. Are you free for the rest of the day?'

'I shall have to go back to the hospital late this evening. Shall we dine somewhere? You're quite comfortable at Brown's?'

'Very comfortable. Could we dine at Claridge's? I've a dress I bought specially for you…'

'I'll see if I can get a table.' He turned round as Beaker came in.

'You had lunch, sir?' Beaker didn't look at Anneliese. When the professor said that, yes, he'd had something, Beaker went on, 'Then I shall bring tea here, sir. A little early, but you may be glad of it.'

'Splendid, Beaker. As soon as you like.' And, when Beaker had gone, the professor said, 'I'll go and phone now…'

He took his bag to his study and pressed the button on the answering machine. There were several calls from when Beaker had been out of the house; the rest he had noted down and put with the letters. The professor leafed through them, listened to the answering machine and booked a table for dinner. He would have liked to dine quietly at home.

They talked trivialities over tea—news from home and friends, places Anneliese had visited. She had no interest in his work save in his successes; his social advancement was all-important to her, although she was careful not to let him see that.

He drove her to Brown's presently, and went back to work at his desk until it was time to dress. Immaculate in black tie, he went to the garage at the end of the mews to get his car, and drove himself to the hotel.

Anneliese wasn't ready. He cooled his heels for fifteen minutes or so before she joined him.

'I've kept you waiting, Ruerd,' she said laughingly. 'But I hope you think it is worth it.'

He assured her that it was, and indeed she made a magnificent picture in a slim sheath of cerise silk, her hair piled high, sandals with four-inch heels and an arm loaded with gold bangles. His ring, a large diamond, glittered on her finger. A ring which she had chosen and which he disliked.

Certainly she was a woman any man would be proud to escort, he told himself. He supposed that he was tired; a good night's sleep was all that was needed. Anneliese looked lovely, and dinner at Claridge's was the very least he could offer her. Tomorrow, he reflected, he would somehow find time to take her out again—dancing, perhaps, at one of the nightclubs. And there was that exhibition of paintings at a gallery in Bond Street if he could manage to find time to take her.

He listened to her chatter as they drove to Claridge's and gave her his full attention. Dinner was entirely satisfactory: admiring looks followed Anneliese as they went to their table, the food was delicious and the surroundings luxurious. As he drove her back she put a hand on his arm.

'A lovely dinner, darling, thank you. I shall do some shopping tomorrow; can you meet me for lunch? And could we go dancing in the evening? We must talk; I've so many plans…'

At the hotel she offered a cheek for his kiss. 'I shall go straight to bed. See you tomorrow.'

The professor got back into his car and drove to the hospital. He wasn't entirely satisfied with the condition of the patient he had seen that afternoon, and he wanted to be sure…

Emmy, sitting before her switchboard, knitting, knew that the professor was there, standing behind her, although he had made no sound. Why is that? she wondered; why should I know that?

His, 'Good evening, Ermentrude,' was uttered quietly. 'You slept well?' he added.

He came to stand beside her now, strikingly handsome in black tie and quite unconscious of it.

'Good evening, sir. Yes, thank you. I hope you had time to rest.'

His mouth twitched. 'I have been dining out. Making conversation, talking of things which don't interest me. If I sound a bad-tempered man who doesn't know when he is lucky, then that is exactly what I am.'

'No, you're not,' said Emmy reasonably. 'You've had a busy day, much busier than anyone else because you've had to make important decisions about your patients. All that's the matter with you is that you are tired. You must go home and have a good night's sleep.'

She had quite forgotten to whom she was speaking. 'I suppose you've come to see that man with the blood clot on the brain?'

He asked with interest, 'Do you know about him?'

'Well, of course I do. I hear things, don't I? And I'm interested.'

She took an incoming telephone call and, when she had dealt with it the professor had gone.

He didn't stop on his way out, nor did he speak, but she was conscious of his passing. She found that disconcerting.

Audrey was punctual and in a peevish mood. 'I had a ticking off,' she told Emmy sourly. 'I don't know why they had to make such a fuss—after all, you were here. No one would have known if it hadn't been for that Professor ter Mennolt being here. Who does he think he is, anyway?'

'He's rather nice,' said Emmy mildly. 'He gave me a lift home.'

'In that great car of his? Filthy rich, so I've heard. Going to marry some Dutch beauty—I was talking to his secretary…'

'I hope they'll be very happy,' said Emmy. A flicker of unhappiness made her frown. She knew very little about the professor and she found him disturbing; a difficult man, a man who went his own way. All the same, she would like him to live happily ever after…

If he came into the hospital during the last nights of her duty, she didn't see him. It wasn't until Sunday morning, when the relief had come to take over and she was free at last to enjoy her two days off, that she met him again as she stood for a moment outside the hospital entrance, taking blissful breaths of morning air, her eyes closed. She was imagining that she was back in the country, despite the petrol fumes.

She opened her eyes, feeling foolish, when the professor observed, 'I am surprised that you should linger, Ermentrude. Surely you must be hellbent on getting away from the hospital as quickly as possible?'

'Good morning, sir,' said Ermentrude politely. 'It's just nice to be outside.' She saw his sweater and casual trousers. 'Have you been here all night?'

'No, no—only for an hour or so.' He smiled down at her. She looked pale with tiredness. Her small nose shone, her hair had been ruthlessly pinned into a bun, very neat and totally without charm. She reminded him of a kitten who had been out all night in the rain. 'I'll drop you off on my way.'

'You're going past my home? Really? Thank you.'

He didn't find it necessary to answer her, but popped her into the car and drove through the almost empty streets. At her door, he said, 'No, don't get out. Give me your key.'

He went and opened the door, and then opened the car door, took her bag from her and followed her inside. George was delighted to see them, weaving round their feet, pushing Snoodles away, giving small, excited barks.

The professor went to open the kitchen door to let both animals out into the garden, and he put the kettle on. For all the world as though he lived here, thought Emmy, and if she hadn't been so tired she would have said so. Instead she stood in the kitchen and yawned.

The professor glanced at her. 'Breakfast,' he said briskly and unbuttoned his coat and threw it over a chair. 'If you'll feed the animals, I'll boil a couple of eggs.'

She did as she was told without demur; she couldn't be bothered to argue with him. She didn't remember asking him to stay for breakfast, but perhaps he was very hungry. She fed the animals and by then he had laid the table after a fashion, made toast and dished up the eggs.

They sat at the table eating their breakfast for all the world like an old married couple. The professor kept up a gentle meandering conversation which required little or no reply, and Emmy, gobbling toast, made very little effort to do so. She was still tired, but the tea and the food had revived her so that presently she said, 'It was very kind of you to get breakfast. I'm very grateful. I was a bit tired.'

'You had a busy week. Will your mother and father return soon?'

'Tomorrow morning.' She gave him an owl-like look. 'I expect you want to go home, sir...'

'Presently. Go upstairs, Ermentrude, take a shower and get into bed. I will tidy up here. When you are in bed I will go home.'

'You can't do the washing up.'

'Indeed I can.' Not quite a lie; he had very occasionally needed to rinse a cup or glass if Beaker hadn't been there.

He made a good job of it, attended to the animals, locked the kitchen door and hung the tea towel to dry, taking his time about it. It was quiet in the house, and presently he went upstairs. He got no answer from his quiet, 'Ermentrude?' but one of the doors on the landing was half-open.

The room was small, nicely furnished and very tidy. Emmy was asleep in her bed, her mouth slightly open, her hair all over the pillow. He thought that nothing short of a brass band giving a concert by her bedside would waken her. He went downstairs again and out of the house, shutting the door behind him.

Driving to Chelsea, he looked at his watch. It would be eleven o'clock before he was home. He was taking Anneliese to lunch with friends, and he suspected that when they returned she would want to make plans for their future. There had been no time so far, and he would be at the hospital for a great deal of the days ahead. He was tired now; Anneliese wasn't content to dine quietly and spend the evening at home and yesterday his day had been full. A day in the country would be delightful...

Beaker came to meet him as he opened his front door. His, 'Good morning, sir,' held faint reproach. 'You were detained at the hospital? I prepared breakfast at the usual time. I can have it on the table in ten minutes.'

'No need, Beaker, thanks. I've had breakfast. I'll have a shower and change, and then perhaps a cup of coffee before Juffrouw van Moule gets here.'

'You breakfasted at the hospital, sir?'

'No, no. I boiled an egg and made some toast and had a pot of strong tea. I took someone home. We were both hungry—it seemed a sensible thing to do.'

Beaker inclined his head gravely. A boiled egg, he re-flected—no bacon, mushrooms, scrambled eggs, as only he, Beaker, could cook them—and strong tea… He sup-pressed a shudder. A small plate of his home-made savoury biscuits, he decided, and perhaps a sandwich with Gentlemen's Relish on the coffee tray.

It was gratifying to see the professor eating the lot when he came downstairs again. He looked as though he could do with a quiet day, reflected his faithful servant, instead of gallivanting off with that Juffrouw van Moule. Beaker hadn't taken to her—a haughty piece, and critical of him. He wished his master a pleasant day in a voice which hinted otherwise. He was informed that Juffrouw van Moule would be returning for tea, and would probably stay for dinner.

Beaker took himself to the kitchen where he unbur-dened himself to his cat, Humphrey, while he set about making the little queen cakes usually appreciated by the professor's lady visitors.

Anneliese looked ravishing, exquisitely made-up, not a hair of her head out of place and wearing a stone-coloured crêpe de chine outfit of deceptive simplicity which screamed money from every seam.

She greeted the professor with a charming smile, offered a cheek with the warning not to disarrange her hair and settled herself in the car.

'At last we have a day together,' she observed. 'I'll come back with you after lunch. That man of yours will give us a decent tea, I suppose. I might even stay for dinner.'

She glanced at his profile. 'We must discuss the future, Ruerd. Where we are to live—we shall have to engage more servants in a larger house, of course, and I suppose you can arrange to give up some of your consultant posts, concentrate on private patients. You have plenty of friends, haven't you? Influential people?'

He didn't look at her. 'I have a great many friends and even more acquaintances,' he told her. 'I have no intention of using them. Indeed, I have no need. Do not expect me to give up my hospital work, though, Anneliese.'

She put a hand on his knee. 'Of course not, Ruerd. I promise I won't say any more about that. But please let us at least discuss finding a larger house where we can entertain. I shall have friends, I hope, and I shall need to return their hospitality.'

She was wise enough to stop then. 'These people we are lunching with—they are old friends?'

'Yes. I knew Guy Bowers-Bentinck before he married. We still see a good deal of each other; he has a charming little wife, Suzannah, and twins—five years old—and a baby on the way.'

'Does she live here, in this village—Great Chisbourne? Does she not find it full? I mean, does she not miss theatres and evenings out and meeting people?'

He said evenly, 'No. She has a husband who loves her, two beautiful children, a delightful home and countless friends. She is content.'

Something in his voice made Anneliese say quickly, 'She sounds delightful; I'm sure I shall like her.'

Which was unfortunately not true. Beneath their socially pleasant manner, they disliked each other heartily— Anneliese because she considered Suzannah to be not worth bothering about, Suzannah because she saw at once that Anneliese wouldn't do for Ruerd at all. She would make him unhappy; surely he could see that for himself?

Lunch was pleasant, Suzannah saw to that—making

small talk while the two men discussed some knotty problem about their work. Anneliese showed signs of boredom after a time; she was used to being the centre of attention and she wasn't getting it. When the men did join in the talk it was about the children eating their meal with them, behaving beautifully.

'Do you have a nursery?' asked Anneliese.

'Oh, yes, and a marvellous old nanny. But the children eat with us unless we're entertaining in the evening. We enjoy their company, and they see more of their father.'

Suzannah smiled across the table at her husband, and Anneliese, looking at him, wondered how such a plain girl could inspire the devoted look he gave her.

She remarked upon it as they drove back to Chelsea. 'Quite charming,' she commented in a voice which lacked sincerity. 'Guy seems devoted to her.'

'Surely that is to be expected of a husband?' the professor observed quietly.

Anneliese gave a little trill of laughter. 'Oh, I suppose so. Not quite my idea of marriage, though. Children should be in the nursery until they go to school, don't you agree?'

He didn't answer that. 'They are delightful, aren't they? And so well behaved.' He sounded remote.

He was going fast on the motorway as the October day faded into dusk. In a few days it would be November, and at the end of that month he would go back to Holland for several weeks, where already a formidable list of consultations awaited him. He would see Anneliese again, of course; she would want to plan their wedding.

When they had first become engaged he had expressed a wish for a quiet wedding and she had agreed. But over the months she had hinted more and more strongly that a big wedding was absolutely necessary: so many friends

and family, and she wanted bridesmaids. Besides, a quiet
wedding would mean she couldn't wear the gorgeous
wedding dress she fully intended to have.

Anneliese began to talk then; she could be very amusing
and she was intelligent. Ruerd wasn't giving her his full
attention, but she was confident that she could alter that.
She embarked on a series of anecdotes about mutual
friends in Holland, taking care not to be critical or spiteful,
only amusing. She knew how to be a charming companion, and felt smug satisfaction when he responded, unaware
that it was only good manners which prompted his replies.

He was tired, he told himself, and Anneliese's chatter
jarred on his thoughts. To talk to her about his work would
have been a relief, to tell her of his busy week at the hospital,
the patients he had seen. But the cursory interest she had
shown when they'd become engaged had evaporated. Not her
fault, of course, but his. He had thought that her interest in
his work was a wish to understand it, but it hadn't been that—
her interest was a social one. To be married to a well-known
medical man with boundless possibilities for advancement.

He slowed the car's speed as they were engulfed in
London's suburbs. She would be a suitable wife—good
looks, a charming manner, clever and always beautifully
turned out.

On aiming back he said, 'We'll have tea round the fire,
shall we? Beaker will have it ready.' He glanced at his watch.
'Rather on the late side, but there's no hurry, is there?'

The sitting room looked warm and welcoming as they
went indoors. Humphrey was sitting before the fire, a small
furry statue, staring at the flames. Anneliese paused
halfway across the room. 'Oh, Ruerd, please get that cat
out of the room. I dislike them, you know—I'm sure
they're not clean, and they shed hairs everywhere.'

The professor scooped Humphrey into his arms. 'He's a well-loved member of my household, Anneliese. He keeps himself cleaner than many humans, and he is brushed so regularly that I doubt if there is a single loose hair.'

He took the cat to the kitchen and sat him down in front of the Aga.

'Juffrouw van Moule doesn't like cats,' he told Beaker in an expressionless voice. 'He'd better stay here until she goes back to the hotel. Could you give us supper about half past eight? Something light; if we're going to have tea now we shan't have much appetite.'

When he went back to the sitting room Anneliese was sitting by the fire. She made a lovely picture in its light, and he paused to look at her as he went in. Any man would be proud to have her as his wife, he reflected, so why was it that he felt no quickening of his pulse at the sight of her?

He brushed the thought aside and sat down opposite her, and watched her pour their tea. She had beautiful hands, exquisitely cared for, and they showed to great advantage as she presided over the tea tray. She looked at him and smiled, aware of the charming picture she made, and presently, confident that she had his attention once more, she began to talk about their future.

'I know we shall see a good deal of each other when you come back to Holland in December,' she began. 'But at least we can make tentative plans.' She didn't wait for his comment but went on, 'I think a summer wedding, don't you? That gives you plenty of time to arrange a long holiday. We might go somewhere for a month or so before settling down.

'Can you arrange it so that you're working in Holland for a few months? You can always fly over here if you're wanted, and surely you can give up your consultancies here after awhile? Private patients, by all means, and, of course, we mustn't lose sight of your friends and colleagues.' She gave him a brilliant smile. 'You're famous here, are you not? It is so important to know all the right people...'

When he didn't reply, she added, 'I am going to be very unselfish and agree to using this house as a London base. Later on perhaps we can find something larger.'

He asked quietly, 'What kind of place had you in mind, Anneliese?'

'I looked in at an estate agent—somewhere near Harrods; I can't remember the name. There were some most suitable flats. Large enough for entertaining. We would need at least five bedrooms—guests, you know—and good servants' quarters.'

Her head on one side, she gave him another brilliant smile. 'Say yes, Ruerd.'

'I have commitments for the next four months here,' he told her, 'and they will be added to in the meantime. In March I've been asked to lecture at a seminar in Leiden, examine students at Groningen and read a paper in Vienna. I cannot give you a definite answer at the moment.'

She pouted. 'Oh, Ruerd, why must you work so hard? At least I shall see something of you when you come back to Holland. Shall you give a party at Christmas?'

'Yes, I believe so. We can talk about that later. Have your family any plans?'

She was still telling him about them when Beaker came to tell them that supper was ready.

Later that evening, as she prepared to go, Anneliese asked, 'Tomorrow, Ruerd? You will be free? We might go to an art exhibition...?'

He shook his head. 'I'm working all day. I doubt if I shall be free before the evening. I'll phone the hotel and leave a message. It will probably be too late for dinner, but we might have a drink.'

She had to be content with that. She would shop, she decided, and dine at the hotel. She was careful not to let him see how vexed she was.

The next morning as the professor made his way through the hospital he looked, as had become his habit, to where Ermentrude sat. She wasn't there, of course.

She was up and dressed, getting the house just so, ready for her mother and father. She had slept long and soundly, and had gone downstairs to find that the professor had left everything clean and tidy in the kitchen. He had left a tea tray ready, too; all she'd needed to do was put on the kettle and make toast.

'Very thoughtful of him,' said Emmy now, to George, who was hovering hopefully for a biscuit. 'You wouldn't think to look at him that he'd know one end of a tea towel from the other. He must have a helpless fiancée...'

She frowned. Even if his fiancée was helpless he could obviously afford to have a housekeeper or at least a daily woman. She fell to wondering about him. When would he be married, have children? Where did he live while he was working in London? And where was his home in Holland? Since neither George nor Snoodles could answer, she put these questions to the back of her mind and turned her thoughts to the shopping she must do before her parents came home.

They knew about the bomb, of course; it had been on TV and in the papers. But when Emmy had phoned her parents she had told them very little about it, and had remained guiltily silent when her mother had expressed her relief that Emmy had been on day duty and hadn't been there. Now that they were home, exchanging news over coffee and biscuits, the talk turned naturally enough to the bomb outrage. 'So fortunate that you weren't there,' said Mrs Foster.

'Well, as a matter of fact, I was,' said Emmy. 'But I was quite all right…' She found herself explaining about Professor ter Mennolt bringing her home and him making tea.

'We are in his debt,' observed her father. 'Although he did only what any decent-thinking person would have done.'

Her mother said artlessly, 'He sounds a very nice man. Is he elderly? I suppose so if he's a professor.'

'Not elderly—not even middle-aged,' said Emmy. 'They say at the hospital that he's going to marry soon. No one knows much about him, and one wouldn't dare ask him.'

She thought privately that one day, if the opportunity occurred, she might do just that. For some reason it was important to her that he should settle down and be happy. He didn't strike her as being happy enough. He ought to be; he was top of his profession, with a girl waiting for him, and presumably enough to live on in comfort.

Her two days went much too quickly. Never mind if it rained for almost all of the time. Her father was away in the day, and she and her mother spent a morning window shopping in Oxford Street, and long hours sitting by the fire—her mother knitting, Emmy busy with the delicate embroidery which she loved to do.

They talked—the chances of her father getting a teaching post near their old home were remote; all the same they discussed it unendingly. 'We don't need a big house,' said her mother. 'And you could come with us, of course, Emmy—there's bound to be some job for you. Or you might meet someone and marry.' She peered at her daughter. 'There isn't anyone here, is there, love?'

'No, Mother, and not likely to be. It would be lovely if Father could get a teaching post and we could sell this house.'

Her mother smiled. 'No neighbours, darling. Wouldn't it be heaven? No rows of little houses all exactly alike. Who knows what is round the corner?'

It was still raining when Emmy set off to work the following morning. The buses were packed and tempers were short. She got off before the hospital stop was reached, tired of being squeezed between wet raincoats and having her feet poked at with umbrellas. A few minutes' walk even on a London street was preferable to strap-hanging.

She was taking a short cut through a narrow lane where most of the houses were boarded up or just plain derelict, when she saw the kitten. It was very small and very wet, sitting by a boarded-up door, and when she went nearer she saw that it had been tied by a piece of string to the door handle. It looked at her and shivered, opened its tiny mouth and mewed almost without sound.

Emmy knelt down, picked it up carefully, held it close and rooted around in her shoulder bag for the scissors she always carried. It was the work of a moment to cut the string, tuck the kitten into her jacket and be on her way once more. She had no idea what she was going to do with the small creature, but to leave it there was unthinkable.

She was early at the hospital; there was time to beg a cardboard box from one of the porters, line it with yesterday's newspaper and her scarf and beg some milk from the head porter.

'You won't 'arf cop it,' he told her, offering a mugful. 'I wouldn't do it for anyone else, Emmy, and mum's the word.' He nodded and winked. She was a nice young lady, he considered, always willing to listen to him telling her about his wife's diabetes.

Emmy tucked the box away at her feet, dried the small creature with her handkerchief, offered it milk and saw with satisfaction that it fell instantly into a refreshing sleep. It woke briefly from time to time, scoffed more milk and dropped off again. Very much to her relief, Emmy got to the end of her shift with the kitten undetected.

She was waiting for her relief when the supervisor bore down upon her, intent on checking and finding fault if she could. It was just bad luck that the kitten should wake at that moment, and, since it was feeling better, it mewed quite loudly.

Meeting the lady's outraged gaze, Emmy said, 'I found him tied to a doorway. In the rain. I'm going to take him home…'

'He has been here all day?' The supervisor's bosom swelled to alarming proportions. 'No animal is allowed inside the hospital. You are aware of that, are you not, Miss Foster? I shall report this, and in the meantime the animal can be taken away by one of the porters.'

'Don't you dare,' said Emmy fiercely. 'I'll not allow it. You are—'

It was unfortunate that she was interrupted before she could finish.

'Ah,' said Professor ter Mennolt, looming behind the supervisor. 'My kitten. Good of you to look after it for me, Ermentrude.' He gave the supervisor a bland smile. 'I am breaking the rules, am I not? But this seemed the best place for it to be until I could come and collect it.'

'Miss Foster has just told me…' began the woman.

'Out of the kindness of her heart,' said the professor outrageously. 'She had no wish to get me into trouble. Isn't that correct, Ermentrude?'

She nodded, and watched while he soothed the supervisor's feelings with a bedside manner which she couldn't have faulted.

'I will overlook your rudeness, Miss Foster,' she said finally, and sailed away.

'Where on earth did you find it?' asked the professor with interest.

She told him, then went on, 'I'll take him home. He'll be nice company for Snoodles and George.'

'An excellent idea. Here is your relief. I shall be outside when you are ready.'

'Why?' asked Emmy.

'You sometimes ask silly questions, Ermentrude. To take you both home.'

Emmy made short work of handing over, got into her mac, picked up the box and went to the entrance. The Bentley was outside, and the professor bundled her and her box into it and drove away in the streaming rain.

The kitten sat up on wobbly legs and mewed. It was bedraggled and thin, and Emmy said anxiously, 'I do hope he'll be all right.'

'Probably a she. I'll look the beast over.'

'Would you? Thank you. Then if it's necessary I'll take him—her—to the vet.' She added uncertainly, 'That's if it's not interfering with whatever you're doing?'

'I can spare half an hour.' He sounded impatient.

She unlocked the door and ushered him into the hall, where he took up so much room she had to sidle past him to open the sitting-room door.

'You're so large,' she told him, and ushered him into the room.

Mrs Foster was sitting reading with Snoodles on her lap. She looked up as they went in and got to her feet.

'I'm sure you're the professor who was so kind to Emmy,' she said, and offered a hand. 'I'm her mother. Emmy, take off that wet mac and put the kettle on, please. What's in the box?'

'A kitten.'

Mrs Foster offered a chair. 'Just like Emmy—always finding birds with broken wings and stray animals.' She smiled from a plain face very like her daughter's, and he thought what a charming woman she was.

'I offered to look at the little beast,' he explained. 'It was tied to a door handle…'

'People are so cruel. But how kind of you. I'll get a clean towel so that we can put the little creature on it while you look. Have a cup of tea first, won't you?'

Emmy came in then, with the tea tray, and they drank their tea while the kitten, still in its box, was put before the fire to warm up. George sat beside it, prepared to be friendly. Snoodles had gone to sit on top of the bookcase, looking suspicious.

Presently, when the kitten had been carefully examined by the professor and pronounced as well as could be expected, he thanked Mrs Foster for his tea with charming good manners, smiled at Emmy and drove himself away.

'I like him,' observed Mrs Foster, shutting the front door.

Emmy, feeding the kitten bread and milk, didn't say anything.

CHAPTER THREE

ANNELIESE found Ruerd absent-minded when they met on the following day—something which secretly annoyed her. No man, she considered, should be that while he was in her company. He was taking her out to dinner, and she had gone to great pains to look her best. Indeed, heads turned as they entered the restaurant; they made a striking couple, and she was aware of that.

She realised very soon that he had no intention of talking about their future. She had a splendid conceit of herself—it never entered her head that the lack of interest could be anything else but a temporary worry about his work—but she had the sense to say no more about her plans for the future, and laid herself out to be an amusing companion.

She considered that she had succeeded too, for as he drove her back to the hotel she suggested that she might stay for several more days, adding prettily, 'I miss you, Ruerd.'

All he said was, 'Why not stay? Perhaps I can get tickets for that show you want to see. I'll do my best to keep my evenings free.'

He drew up before the hotel and turned to look at her. She looked lovely in the semi-shadows, and he bent to kiss her.

She put up a protesting hand. 'Oh, darling, not now. You always disarrange my hair.'

He got out, opened her door, went with her into the foyer, bade her goodnight with his beautiful manners and drove himself back home, reminding himself that Anneliese was the ideal wife for him. Her coolness was something he would overcome in time. She was beautiful, he told himself, and she knew how to dress, how to manage his large household in Holland, how to be an amusing and charming companion…

He let himself into his house and Beaker and Humphrey came into the hall.

'A pleasant evening, I trust, sir?' asked Beaker smoothly.

The professor nodded absently. Humphrey had reminded him about the kitten and Ermentrude. He frowned; the girl had a habit of popping into his thoughts for no reason. He must remember to ask about the kitten if he saw her in the morning.

Emmy, still refreshed by her days off, was a little early. She settled down before the switchboard, arranged everything just as she liked it and took out her knitting. She was halfway through the first row when she became aware that the professor was there. She turned to look at him and, since it was a crisp autumn morning and the sun was shining and she was pleased to see him, she smiled widely and wished him good morning.

His reply was cool. He took his spectacles out of his pocket, polished them and put them on his commanding nose in order to read the variety of notes left for him at the desk.

Emmy's smile dwindled. She turned back and picked up her knitting and wished that she were busy. Perhaps she shouldn't have spoken to him. She was only being civil.

'It's Friday morning,' she said in a reasonable voice, 'and the sun's shining.'

He took his specs off, the better to stare down at her.

'The kitten—is it thriving?'

'Yes. Oh, yes, and Snoodles and George are so kind to it. Snoodles washes it and it goes to sleep with them. It's a bit of a squash in their basket.' She beamed at him. 'How nice of you to ask, sir.'

He said testily, 'Nice, nice…a useless word. You would do well to enlarge your knowledge of the English language, Ermentrude.'

'That is very rude, Professor,' said Emmy coldly, and was glad that there was a call which kept her busy for a few moments. Presently she turned her head cautiously. The professor had gone.

I shall probably get the sack, she reflected. The idea hung like a shadow over her for the rest of the day. By the time she was relieved, Authority hadn't said anything, but probably in the morning there would be a letter waiting for her, giving her a month's notice.

She went slowly to the entrance, wondering if a written apology to the professor would be a good idea. She began to compose it in her head, pausing on her way to get the words right so that the professor had plenty of time to overtake her as she crossed the entrance hall. He came to a halt in front of her so that she bounced against his waistcoat. Emmy, being Emmy, said at once, 'I'm composing a letter of apology to you, sir, although I really don't see why I should.'

'I don't see why you should either,' he told her. 'What were you going to put in it?'

'Well—"Dear sir", of course, to start with, and then something about being sorry for my impertinence.'

'You consider that you were impertinent?' he wanted to know.

'Good heavens, no, but if I don't apologise I dare say I'll get the sack for being rude or familiar or something.'

She received an icy stare. 'You have a poor opinion of me, Ermentrude.'

She made haste to put things right. 'No, no, I think you are very nice…' She paused. 'Oh, dear, I'll have to think of another word, won't I?' She smiled at him, ignoring the cold eyes. 'But you are nice! I suppose I could call you handsome or sexy…'

He held up a large hand. 'Spare my blushes, Ermentrude. Let us agree, if possible, on nice. I can assure you, though, that you are in no danger of being dismissed.'

'Oh, good. The money's useful at home, you know.'

Which presumably was why she was dressed in less than eye-catching fashion.

'The matter being cleared up, I'll drive you home. It's on my way.'

'No, it's not. Thank you very much, though; I can catch a bus…'

The professor, not in the habit of being thwarted, took her arm and walked her through the door.

In the car he asked, 'What are you doing with your evening? Meeting the boyfriend, going to a cinema, having a meal?'

She glanced at him. He was looking ahead, not smiling.

'Me? Well, I haven't got a boyfriend, so I won't be going to the cinema or out for a meal. Mother and Father are home, so we'll have supper and take George for a walk and see to Snoodles and the kitten. And we'll talk…' She added, 'We like talking.'

When he didn't answer she asked, 'Are you going to have a pleasant evening, Professor?'

'I am taking my finacée to Covent Garden to the ballet, and afterwards we shall have supper somewhere. I do not care for the ballet.'

'Well, no, I dare say men don't. But supper will be fun—especially as it's with your fiancée. Somewhere nice—I mean, fashionable…'

'Indeed, yes.'

Something in his voice made her ask, 'Don't you like going out to supper, either?' She wanted to ask about his fiancée but she didn't dare—besides, the thought of him getting married made her feel vaguely unhappy.

'It depends where it is eaten and with whom. I would enjoy taking a dog for a long walk in one of the parks and eating my supper…' He paused. 'Afterwards.' Which hadn't been what he had wanted to say.

'That's easy. Get a dog. You could both take it for a walk in the evenings and then go home and have a cosy supper together.'

The professor envisaged Anneliese tramping round Hyde Park and then returning to eat her supper in his company. No dressing up, no waiters, no other diners to admire her—his mind boggled.

He said slowly, 'I will get a dog. From Battersea Dogs Home. Will you come with me and help me choose him, Ermentrude?'

'Me? I'd love to, but what about your fiancée?'

'She returns to Holland in a few days.'

'Oh, well, all right. It'll be a lovely surprise for her when she comes back to see you again.'

'It will certainly be a surprise,' said the professor.

He dropped her off at her house with a casual nod and a goodnight, and began to drive to his own home. I must be out of my mind, he reflected. Anneliese will never agree to a dog, and certainly not to long walks with it. What is it about Ermentrude which makes me behave with such a lack of good sense? And why do I enjoy being with her when I have Anneliese?

Later that evening, after the ballet, while they were having supper, he deliberately talked about Ermentrude, telling Anneliese something of the bomb scare, mentioning the kitten.

Anneliese listened smilingly. 'Darling, how like you to bother about some little girl just because she got scared with that bomb. She sounds very dull. Is she pretty?'

'No.'

'I can just imagine her—plain and mousy and badly dressed. Am I right?'

'Yes. She has a pretty voice, though. A useful attribute in her particular job.'

'I hope she's grateful to you. I mean, for a girl like that it must be a great uplift to be spoken to by you.'

The professor said nothing to that. He thought it unlikely that Ermentrude had experienced any such feeling. Her conversation had been invariably matter-of-fact and full of advice. As far as she was concerned he was just another man.

He smiled at the thought, and Anneliese said, 'Shall we talk about something else? I find this girl a bit boring.'

Never that, thought the professor. Though unable to hold a candle to Anneliese's beauty. If circumstances had not thrown them together briefly, he would never have noticed her. All the same he smiled a little, and Anneliese, despite feeling quite confident of Ruerd's regard for her, decided there and then to do something about it.

* * *

Emmy told her mother and father about going to Battersea Dogs Home with the professor.

'When does the professor intend to marry?' asked her mother.

'I've no idea. He doesn't talk about it, and I couldn't ask him. We only talk about things which don't matter.' She sighed. 'I expect he'll tell me when he's got the time to choose a dog.'

But although he wished her good morning and good evening each day, that was all. He didn't ask after the kitten either.

It was towards the end of the next week when Emmy came back from her dinner break and found someone waiting for her. After one look she knew who it was: the professor's fiancée; she had to be. He would, she thought, decide for nothing less than this beautiful creature with the perfect hairdo and the kind of clothes any woman could see at a glance had cost a small fortune.

She said, 'Can I help? Do you want the professor?'

'You know who I am?'

Emmy said diffidently, 'Well, not exactly, but Professor ter Mennolt mentioned that his fiancée was staying in London and—and you're exactly how I imagined you would be.'

'And what was that?' Anneliese sounded amused.

'Quite beautiful and splendidly dressed.' Emmy smiled. 'I'll show you where you can wait while I try and get him for you.'

'Oh, I don't wish to see him. He was telling me about the bomb scare here and what an unpleasant experience it was for everyone. He told me about you, too.' She gave a little laugh. 'I would have known you anywhere from his description—plain and mousy and badly dressed. Oh, dear, I shouldn't have said that. Forgive me—my silly tongue.'

Emmy said quietly, 'Yes, that's a very good description of me, isn't it? Are you enjoying your visit? London in the autumn is rather special.'

'The shopping is good, and we enjoy going out in the evenings. Do you go out much?'

Her voice, too loud and with a strong accent, grated on Emmy's ears.

'Not very much. It's quite a long day here. When I do go home I walk our dog…'

'You have a dog? I do not like them, and certainly not in the house. I dislike cats also—their hairs…'

Emmy's relief telephonist was showing signs of impatience, which made it easy for her to say that she had to return to her switchboard.

'It's been nice meeting you,' said Emmy mendaciously. For once she agreed with the professor that 'nice' was a useless word and quite inappropriate. She hoped that she would never see the girl again.

'I won't keep you from your work. It was most satisfying to find that Ruerd's description of you was so accurate.'

Anneliese didn't offer a hand, nor did she say goodbye. Emmy and the relief watched her go.

'Who's she?'

'Professor ter Mennolt's fiancée.'

'The poor man. She'll lead him a dance; you see if she doesn't.'

'She's very beautiful,' said Emmy, in a voice which conveyed nothing of her feelings. Though her goodnight in reply to the professor's passing greeting was austere in the extreme.

The following evening, after a wakeful night, and a different day, it held all the hauteur of royalty in a rage.

Not that the professor appeared to notice. 'I'm free on Sunday. Will you help me choose a dog—some time in the morning—or afternoon if you prefer?'

He didn't sound friendly; he sounded like someone performing an obligation with reluctance. 'My fiancée has gone back to Holland this morning,' he added inconsequentially.

'No,' said Emmy coldly. 'I'm afraid I can't.'

He eyed her narrowly. 'Ah, of course—you consider it very incorrect of me to spend a few hours with someone other than Anneliese. The moment she sets foot in the plane, too.'

'No. At least partly.' She frowned. 'It was the bomb which…' she sought for the right words '…was the reason for you speaking to me. In such circumstances that was natural. There is no need—'

He said silkily, 'My dear Emmy, you do not for one moment imagine that you are a serious rival to Anneliese? For God's sake, all I have asked of you is to help me choose a dog.'

'What a silly thing to say,' said Emmy roundly. 'It is the last thing I would think. I am, as you so clearly described me, plain and mousy and badly dressed. Certainly no companion for you, even at a dogs' home!'

He said slowly, 'When did you meet Anneliese?'

'She came here to see me. She wanted to see if you had described me accurately.' Emmy added stonily, 'You had.'

The professor stood looking at her for a long minute. He said, 'I'm sorry, Ermentrude, it was unpardonable of me to discuss you with Anneliese and I had no idea that she had come here to see you.'

'Well,' said Emmy matter-of-factly, 'it's what any woman would do—you could have been lying about me.' She gave a rueful smile. 'I might have been a gorgeous blonde.'

'I do not lie, Ermentrude. I will not lie to you now and tell you that you are neither mousy nor plain nor badly dressed. You are a very nice—and I use the word in its correct sense—person, and I apologise for hurting you. One day someone—a man—will look at you and love you. He won't notice the clothes; he will see only your lovely eyes and the kindness in your face. He will find you beautiful and tell you so.'

Emmy said, 'Pigs might fly, but it's kind of you to say so. It doesn't matter, you know. I've known since I was a little girl that I had no looks to speak of. It's not as though I'm surprised.' She gave a very small sigh. 'Your Anneliese is very beautiful, and I hope you'll be very happy with her.'

The professor remained silent and she put through an outside call. He was still there when she had done it.

He was not a man in the habit of asking a favour twice, but he did so now.

'Will you help me choose a dog, Ermentrude?'

She turned to look at him. 'Very well, Professor. In the afternoon, if you don't mind. About two o'clock?'

'Thank you. I'll call for you then.'

He went away, and just for a while she was too busy to reflect over their conversation. Which was a good thing, she decided, for her bottled up feelings might spill over. She would go with him on Sunday, but after that good morning and good evening would be sufficient.

Later, when she considered she had cooled down enough to think about it, she thought that it wasn't that he had discussed her with Anneliese so much as the fact that he hadn't denied calling her plain which had made her angry. On the other hand, supposing he had denied it—and she'd known that he was lying? Would she have been just as angry? In all fairness to him she thought that she would. She liked him even if there was no reason to do so.

* * *

Her mother and father, when she told them on Sunday answered exactly as she had known they would. Her mother said, 'Wear a warm coat, dear, it gets chilly in the afternoons.'

Her father said, 'Good idea—enjoy yourself, Emmy!'

Her parents were going to Coventry on the following day—the last week away from home, her mother assured her, for her father would be round and about London after that. 'You're sure you don't mind?' she asked anxiously. 'I know you're busy all day, but it's lonely for you, especially in the evenings.'

'Mother, I've heaps to do, honestly, and I'll get the garden tidied up for the winter.' Though the garden was a miserably small patch of grass surrounded by narrow flowerbeds which Emmy would hopefully plant.

The professor arrived punctually, exchanged suitable and civil remarks with her mother and father and ushered Emmy into the car. She had gone to great pains to improve her appearance. True, her jacket and skirt were off the peg, bought to last, and therefore a useful brown—a colour which didn't suit her. But the cream blouse under the jacket was crisp, and her gloves and shoulder bag were leather, elderly but well cared for. Since her brown shoes were well-worn loafers, she had borrowed a pair of her mother's. Court shoes with quite high heels. They pinched a bit, but they looked all right.

The professor, eyeing her unobtrusively, was surprised to find himself wishing that some fairy godmother would wave a wand over Emmy and transform the brown outfit into something pretty. He was surprised, too, that she wore her clothes with an air—when he had thought about it, and that hadn't been often, he had supposed that she had little interest in clothes. He saw now that he was wrong.

He made casual conversation as he drove, and Emmy replied cautiously, not at all at her ease, wishing she hadn't come. Once they had reached the dogs' home she forgot all about that. She had never seen so many dogs, nor heard such a concert of barking.

They went to and fro looking at doggy faces, some pressed up to the front of their shelters, eager for attention, others sitting indifferently at the back. 'They're pretending that they don't mind if no one wants them,' said Emmy. 'I wish we could have them all.'

The professor smiled down at her. Her face was alight with interest and compassion and, rather to his surprise, didn't look in the least plain.

'I'm afraid one is the best I can do. Have you seen a dog which you think might suit me? There are so many, I have no preference at the moment.'

They had stopped in front of a shelter to watch the antics of an overgrown puppy, chosen by a family of children and expressing his delight. There were a lot of dogs; Emmy looked at them all and caught the eye of a large woolly dog with the kindly face of a labrador and a tremendous sweeping tail. He was sitting in the corner, and it was obvious to her that he was too proud to attract attention. Only his eyes begged her...

'That one,' said Emmy. 'There.'

The professor studied the dog. 'Yes,' he said. 'That's the one.'

The dog couldn't have heard them, but he came slowly to the front of the shelter and wagged his tail, staring up at them. When, after the necessary formalities had been gone through, the professor fastened a new collar round the dog's powerful neck, he gave a small, happy bark.

'You see?' said Emmy. 'He knew you'd have him. He's so lovely. Did they say what breed he was?'

'Well, no. There is some uncertainty. He was left to fend for himself until some kind soul brought him here. He's been here for some time. He's rather on the large side for the average household.'

They got into the car, and the dog settled warily on a blanket on the back seat.

'You do like him?' Emmy asked anxiously.

'Yes. An instant rapport. I can only hope that Beaker will feel the same way.'

'Beaker?'

'Yes, my man. He runs the house for me. Did I mention him when I told you about Humphrey? He's a splendid fellow.'

He drew up in front of his house and Emmy said, 'Oh, is this where you live? It's not like London at all, is it? Is there a garden?'

'Yes—come and see it?'

'I'd like to, but you'll have a lot to do with the dog, and you have a day off today, too, haven't you?'

He said gravely that, yes, he had, but he was doing nothing else with it. 'So please come in and meet Beaker and Humphrey and help me to get this beast settled in.'

Beaker, opening the door, did no more than lift a dignified eyebrow at the sight of the dog. He bowed gravely to Emmy and shook the hand she offered. 'A handsome beast,' he pronounced. 'Straight into the garden, sir?'

'Yes, Beaker. He's been at the home for a long time so he's a bit uncertain about everything. Ten minutes in the garden may help. Then tea, if you please.'

Beaker slid away and the professor led Emmy across the hall, into the sitting room and out of the French window into the garden. For London it was quite large, with a high brick wall and one or two trees—a mountain ash, a small silver birch, bare of leaves now, and a very old apple tree.

The dog needed no urging to explore, and Emmy said, 'Oh, how delightful. It must look lovely in the spring— lots of bulbs?'

When he nodded, watching her face, she added, 'And an apple tree. We used to have several…'

'You had a large garden?' he asked gently.

'Yes. A bit rambling, but everything grew. It was heaven to go out in the morning. And the air—there isn't much air here, is there? Well, not around St Luke's.' She turned away, annoyed with herself for saying so much, as though she had asked to be pitied. 'What will you call him?'

'I was hoping you would think of a name.'

'Something dignified and a bit regal to make up for his unhappy life.' She thought about it. 'No, it should be a name that sounds as though he's one of the family. Charlie— when I was a little girl I wanted a brother called Charlie.'

'Charlie it shall be.' The professor called the dog, and he came at once, lolloping across the lawn, his tongue hanging out, his preposterous tail waving.

'You see?' said Emmy happily. 'He knows.'

The professor put a gentle hand on Charlie's woolly head. 'I think he has earned his tea, don't you? Let us go indoors; we've earned ours, too.'

'Oh, well,' said Emmy. 'I didn't mean to stay, only to see your garden.'

'Charlie and I will be deeply offended if you don't stay for tea. What is more, Beaker will think his efforts aren't sufficiently tempting.'

Not meaning to, she smiled at him. 'Tea would be very nice.'

They had it in the sitting room, sitting by the fire with Beaker's efforts on a low table between them. Tiny sandwiches, fairy cakes, a chocolate cake and miniature macaroons, flanked by a silver teapot and paper-thin china cups and saucers.

Charlie, mindful of his manners, sat himself carefully down before the fire, hopeful eyes on the cake. Presently Beaker opened the door and Humphrey came in, circled the room slowly and finally sat down beside Charlie. He ignored the dog and stared into the flames, and Emmy said anxiously, 'Will they get on, do you think?'

'Yes. Humphrey has no intention of losing face, though. Charlie will have to play second fiddle.'

'Oh, well, I don't suppose he'll mind now he has a family of his own. Will your fiancée like him?'

The professor bit into some cake. 'No. I'm afraid not.'

When Emmy looked concerned he added, 'I spend a good deal of the year in Holland and, of course, Charlie will stay here with Beaker.'

She poured second cups. 'Do you have a dog in Holland?'

'Two. A Jack Russell and an Irish wolfhound.'

She wanted to ask him about his home in Holland, but although he was friendly he was also aloof. Emmy, willing and eager to be friends with everyone, found that daunting. Besides, she wasn't sure what to make of him. In his company she was happy even when they weren't on the best of terms, but away from him, looking at him from a distance as it were, she told herself that there was no point in continuing their friendship—if it could be called that.

Tea finished, she said a little shyly, 'I think I had better go home, Professor. Mother and Father are going to Coventry in the morning. It will be Father's last job away from home.'

'He enjoys his work?' the professor asked idly.

'He'd rather be a schoolmaster, and not in London.'

'If he were to get a post in the country, you would go with your parents?'

'Yes, oh, yes. I expect I'd have to look for another kind of job. I like needlework and sewing. I expect I could find work in a shop or helping a dressmaker.' She added defiantly, 'I like clothes…'

He prudently kept silent about that. He had a brief memory of Anneliese, exquisitely turned out in clothes which must have cost what to Emmy would have been a small fortune. Emmy, he reflected, would look almost pretty if she were to dress in the same way as Anneliese dressed.

He didn't ask her to stay, but waited while she said goodbye to Charlie and Humphrey and thanked Beaker for her tea, and then went with her to the car.

The streets were almost empty on a late Sunday afternoon and the journey didn't take long. At the house he declined her hesitant offer to go in. He opened her door, thanked her for her help, still standing on the pavement in the dull little street, and waited while she opened the house door and went inside.

Driving back home, he reflected that he had enjoyed his afternoon with Emmy. She was a good companion; she didn't chat and she was a good listener, and when she did have something to say it was worth listening to. He must remember to let her know from time to time how Charlie progressed.

A pleasant afternoon, Emmy told her parents, and the dog, Charlie, was just what she would have chosen for herself. 'And I had a lovely tea,' she told them. 'The professor has a man who runs his home for him and makes the most delicious cakes.'

'A nice house?' asked her mother.

Emmy described it—what she had seen of it—and the garden as well.

'It's not like London,' she told them. 'In the garden you might be miles away in the country.'

'You miss our old home, don't you, Emmy?' her father asked.

'Yes, I do, but we're quite cosy here.' Empty words which neither of them believed.

'I dare say the professor will tell you how the dog settles down,' observed her mother.

'Perhaps.' Emmy sounded doubtful.

She didn't see him for several days, and when he at length stopped to speak to her on his way home one evening, it was only to tell her that Charlie was nicely settled in.

'A very biddable animal,' he told her. 'Goes everywhere with me.'

He bade her good evening in a frosty voice and went away, leaving her wondering why he was so aloof.

He's had a busy day, reflected Emmy, he'll be more friendly in the morning.

Only in the morning he wasn't there. Audrey, who always knew the latest gossip, told her as she took over that he had gone to Birmingham.

'Gets around, doesn't he? Going back to Holland for Christmas too. Shan't see much of him—not that he's exactly friendly. Well, what do you expect? He's a senior consultant and no end of a big noise.'

Which was, Emmy conceded, quite true. And a good reason for remembering that next time he might pause for a chat. He was beginning to loom rather large on the edge of her dull, humdrum life, which wouldn't do at all. Sitting there at her switchboard, she reminded herself that they had nothing in common— Well, Charlie perhaps, and being in the hospital when the bomb went off.

Besides, she reminded herself bitterly, he considered her plain and dowdy. If I could spend half as much on myself as that Anneliese of his, reflected Emmy waspishly, I'd show him that I'm not in the least dowdy, and a visit to a beauty salon would work wonders even with a face like mine.

Since neither of their wishes were likely to be fulfilled, she told herself to forget the professor; there were plenty of other things to think about.

It was a pity that she couldn't think of a single one of them—within minutes he was back in her thoughts, making havoc of her good resolutions.

She was in the professor's thoughts too, much to his annoyance. The tiresome girl, he reflected, and why do I have this urge to do something to improve her life? For all I know she is perfectly content with the way she lives. She is young; she could get a job wherever she wishes, buy herself some decent clothes, meet people, find a boyfriend. All of which was nonsense, and he knew it. She deserved better, he considered, a home and work away from London and that pokey little house.

But even if she had the chance to change he knew that she wouldn't leave her home. He had liked her parents; they had fallen on bad times through no fault of her father. Of course, if he could get a post as a schoolmaster again away from London that would solve the problem. Ermentrude could leave St Luke's and shake the dust of London from her well-polished but well-worn shoes.

The professor put down the notes he was studying, took

off his spectacles, polished them and put them back onto his nose. He would miss her.

'This is ridiculous,' he said to himself. 'I don't even know the girl.'

He forebore from adding that he knew Ermentrude as if she were himself, had done since he had first seen her. He was going to marry Anneliese, he reminded himself, and Ermentrude had demonstrated often enough that she had no interest in him. He was too old for her, and she regarded him in a guarded manner which made it plain that in her eyes he was no more than someone she met occasionally at work...

The professor was an honourable man; he had asked Anneliese to marry him—not loving her but knowing that she would make a suitable wife—and there was no possible reason to break his word. Even if Ermentrude loved him, something which was so unlikely that it was laughable.

He gave his lectures, dealt with patients he had been asked to see, arranged appointments for the future and always at the back of his mind was Ermentrude. She would never be his wife but there was a good deal he could do to make her life happier, and, when he got back once more to Chelsea, he set about doing it.

CHAPTER FOUR

DESPITE her resolutions, Emmy missed the professor. She had looked forward to seeing him going to and fro at St Luke's, even if he took no notice of her. He was there, as it were, and she felt content just to know that he was. Of course, she thought about him. She thought about Anneliese too, doubtless getting ready for a grand wedding, spending money like water, secure in the knowledge that she was going to marry a man who could give her everything she could want.

'I only hope she deserves it,' said Emmy, talking to herself and surprising the porter who had brought her coffee.

'If it's women you're talking about, love, you can take it from me they don't deserve nothing. Take my word for it; I'm a married man.'

'Go on with you!' said Emmy. 'I've seen your wife, she's pretty, and you've got that darling baby.'

'I could have done worse.' He grinned at her. 'There's always an exception to every rule, so they say.'

'No sign of our handsome professor,' said Audrey when she came on duty. 'Having fun in Birmingham, I shouldn't wonder. Won't be able to do that once he's a married man, will he? Perhaps he's going straight over to Holland and not coming back here until after Christmas.'

'Christmas is still six weeks away.'

'Don't tell me that he can't do what he chooses when he wants to.'

'I think that if he has patients and work here he'll stay until he's no longer needed. I know you don't like him, but everyone else does.'

'Including you,' said Audrey with a snigger.

'Including me,' said Emmy soberly.

Emmy was on night duty again. Her mother was home and so was her father, now inspecting various schools in outer London and coming home tired each evening. He didn't complain, but the days were long and often unsatisfactory. He had been told that the man he had replaced would be returning to work within a week or ten days, which meant that he would be returning to his badly paid teaching post. Thank heaven, he thought, that Emmy had her job too. Somehow they would manage.

Emmy had dealt with the usual early enquiries, and except for internal calls the evening was quiet. She took out her knitting—a pullover for her father's Christmas present—and began the complicated business of picking up stitches around the neck. She was halfway round it when she became aware of the professor standing behind her. Her hand jerked and she dropped a clutch of stitches.

'There, look what you've made me do!' she said, and turned round to look at him.

'You knew that I was here?' He sounded amused. 'But I hadn't spoken…'

'No, well—I knew there was someone.' She was mumbling, not looking at him now, remembering all at once that what was fast becoming friendship must be nipped in the bud.

She began to pick up the dropped stitches, and wished that the silent switchboard would come alive. Since he just stood there, apparently content with the silence, she asked in a polite voice, 'I hope that Charlie is well, sir?'

The professor, equally polite, assured her that his dog was in excellent health, and registered the 'sir' with a rueful lift of the eyebrows.

'Your kitten?' he asked in his turn.

'Oh, he's splendid, and George and Snoodles take such care of him.'

The professor persevered. 'Has he a name?'

'Enoch. Mother had a cat when she was a little girl called Enoch, and now he's clean and brushed he's the same colour. Ginger with a white waistcoat.' She added, 'Sir.'

The professor saw that he was making no headway; Ermentrude was making it plain that she was being polite for politeness' sake. Apparently she had decided that their friendship, such as it was, was to go no further. Just as well, he reflected, I'm getting far too interested in the girl. He bade her a cool goodnight and went away, and Emmy picked up her knitting once more.

A most unsatisfactory meeting, she reflected. On the other hand it had been satisfactory, hadn't it? She had let him see that their casual camaraderie had been just that—casual, engendered by circumstances. He was shortly going to be married, she reminded herself; he would become immersed in plans for his wedding with Anneliese.

She was mistaken in this. The professor was immersed in plans, but not to do with his future. The wish to transform

Emmy's dull life into one with which she would be happy had driven him to do something about it.

He had friends everywhere; it wasn't too difficult to meet a man he had known at Cambridge and who was now headmaster of a boys' prep school in Dorset. The professor was lucky: a schoolmaster had been forced to leave owing to ill health and there was, he was told cautiously, a vacancy. 'But for the right man. I've only your word for it that this Foster's OK.'

The headmaster wrote in his notebook and tore out the page. 'He can give me a ring...'

The professor shook his head. 'That wouldn't do. If he or his daughter discovered that I was behind it, he'd refuse at once.'

'Got a daughter, has he? Thought you were getting married.'

The professor smiled. 'You can rule out any romantic thoughts, but I would like to help her get out of a life she isn't enjoying; away from London. To do that her father must get a post somewhere in the country, for that's where she belongs.'

His friend sighed. 'Tell you what I'll do. I'll concoct a tale, you know the kind of thing—I'd met someone who knew someone who knew this Foster, and as there was a vacancy et cetera... Will that do? But remember, Ruerd, if I contract any one of these horrible conditions you're so famous for treating, I shall expect the very best treatment—free!'

'A promise I hope I shall never need to keep.' They shook hands, and his friend went home and told his wife that Ruerd ter Mennolt seemed to be putting himself to a great deal of trouble for some girl or other at St Luke's.

'I thought he was marrying that Anneliese of his?'

'And still is, it seems. He was always a man to help lame dogs over stiles.'

'Anneliese doesn't like dogs,' said his wife.

It was the very next day when the letter arrived, inviting Mr Foster to present himself for an interview. And it couldn't have come at a better time, for with the same post came a notice making him redundant from his teaching post on the first of December. They sat over their supper, discussing this marvellous stroke of luck.

'Though we mustn't count our chickens before they are hatched,' said Mr Foster. 'How fortunate that I have Thursday free; I'll have to go by train.'

Emmy went into the kitchen and took the biscuit tin down from the dresser-shelf and counted the money inside. It was money kept for emergencies, and this was an emergency of the best kind.

'Will there be a house with the job?' she asked. 'Littleton Mangate—that's a small village, isn't it? Somewhere in the Blackmore Vale.' She smiled widely. 'Oh, Father, it's almost too good to be true…'

'So we mustn't bank on it until I've had my interview, Emmy. Once that's over and I've been appointed we can make plans.'

The next day, replying sedately to the professor's grave greeting, Emmy almost choked in her efforts not to tell him about the good news. Time enough, she told herself, when her father had got the job. Only then, too, if he asked her.

'Which he won't,' she told George as she brushed him before taking him on his evening trot.

The professor, it seemed, was reluctant as she was to resume their brief conversations. He never failed to greet her if he should pass the switchboard, but that was all. She felt bereft and vaguely resentful, which, seeing that she had wanted it that way, seemed rather hard on him. But at least it boosted her resolve to forget him. Something not easily done since she saw him willy-nilly on most days.

Her father, in his best suit, a neatly typed CV in his coat pocket, left on Thursday morning on an early train, leaving Emmy to fidget through her day's work, alternately positive that her father would get the post and then plunged into despair because he had been made redundant, and finding a job would be difficult, perhaps impossible. In a moment of rare self-pity she saw herself sitting in front of the switchboard for the rest of her working life.

The professor, catching sight of her dejected back view, was tempted to stop and speak to her, but he didn't. A helping hand was one thing, getting involved with her spelt danger. It was a good thing, he reflected, that he would be going over to Holland shortly. He must see as much of Anneliese as possible.

The bus ride home that evening took twice as long as usual, or so it seemed to Emmy. She burst into the house at length and rushed into the kitchen.

Her mother and father were there, turning to look at her with happy faces. 'You've got it,' said Emmy. 'I knew you would, Father. I can't believe it.'

She flung her coat onto a chair, poured herself a cup of tea from the pot and said, 'Tell me all about it. Is there a house? When do you start? Did you like the headmaster?'

'I've been accepted,' said Mr Foster. 'But my references still have to be checked. There's a house, a very nice one, a converted lodge in the school grounds. I am to take over as soon as possible as they are short of a form master. There are still three weeks or so of the term.'

'So you'll be going in a day or two? And Mother? Is the house furnished?'

'No. Curtains and carpets…'

Mr Foster added slowly, 'Your Mother and I have been talking it over. You will have to give a month's notice, will you not? Supposing we have as much furniture as possible sent to Dorset, would you stay on for the last month, Emmy? Could you bear to do that? We'll take George and Snoodles and Enoch with us. The house can be put up for sale at once. There's little chance of it selling quickly, but one never knows. Could you do that? In the meantime your mother will get the house at Littleton Mangate habitable. We can spend Christmas together…'

Emmy agreed at once. She didn't much like the idea of living alone in a half-empty house, but it would be for a few weeks, no more. The idea of leaving St Luke's gave her a lovely feeling of freedom.

'Money?' she asked.

'The bank will give me a loan against this house.' Her father frowned. 'This isn't an ideal arrangement, Emmy, but we really haven't much choice. If you give a month's notice you'll be free by Christmas, and in the meantime there is always the chance that the house will sell.'

'I think that's a splendid idea, Father. When do you start? Almost at once? Mother and I can start packing up and she can join you in a few days. I'll only need a bed and a table and chairs. There's that man—Mr Stokes—at the end of the street. He does removals.'

'I'm not sure that we should leave you,' said her mother worriedly. 'You're sure you don't mind? We can't think what else to do. There's so little time.'

'I'll be quite all right, Mother. It's for such a short time anyway. It's all so exciting…'

They spent the rest of the evening making lists, deciding what to take and what to leave. Tired and excited by the time she got to her bed, Emmy's last waking thought was that once she had left St Luke's she would never see the professor again.

Going to work the next morning, she thought that perhaps she would tell him of the unexpected change in her life.

However, he didn't give her the chance. Beyond an austere good morning he had nothing to say to her, and later, when he left the hospital, he had a colleague with him.

Oh, well, said Emmy to herself, I can always tell him tomorrow.'

Only he wasn't there in the morning; it wasn't until the day was half-done that she heard that he had gone to Holland.

She told herself that it didn't matter at all, that there was no reason to expect him to be interested in her future. She had already given in her notice and would not tell anyone about it.

Back home that evening, she found her mother already busy, turning out drawers and cupboards. 'Your father's arranged for Mr Stokes to collect the furniture in three days' time.' She beamed at Emmy. 'Oh, darling, it's all so wonderful. I don't believe it. Your father is so happy; so am I. It is a great pity that you can't come with us. I hate the idea of you being here on your own.'

Emmy, wrapping up the best china in newspaper and stowing it carefully in a tea chest, paused to say, 'Don't worry Mother. I'll be working all day, and by the time I get back here and have a meal it'll be time to go to bed—the days will fly by. Won't it be lovely having Christmas away from here?'

Her mother paused in stacking books. 'You've hated it here, haven't you, darling? So have I—so has your father. But we can forget all this once we're at Littleton Mangate. Just think, too, when we've sold this house there'll be some money to spend. Enough for you to go to a school of embroidery or whatever else you want to do. You'll meet people of your own age, too.'

Emmy nodded and smiled and, much against her will, thought about the professor.

He, too, was thinking about her, not wishing to but unable to prevent his thoughts going their own way. It was easier to put her to the back of his head while he was at the various hospitals—Leiden, the Hague, Amsterdam, Rotterdam. There were patients for him in all of these, and he was able to dismiss any thoughts other than those to do with his work while he was in the hospitals consulting, examining, deciding on treatment, seeing, in some cases, anxious relations and reassuring patients.

His days were long and busy but when he drove himself home each evening he had time to think. Anneliese was in France, but she would be back soon and he would spend his leisure with her. But in the meantime his time was his own.

Each evening he turned into the drive leading to his house and sighed with content at the sight of it. It was on the edge of a village, a stately old house behind the dunes, the North sea stretching away to the horizon, magnificent stretch of sand sweeping into the distance, north and south. The house had been built by his great-great-grandfather, and was a solid edifice, secure against the bitter winter winds, its rooms large, the windows tall and narrow, and the front door solid enough to withstand a seige.

Ruerd had been born there, and between schools, universities and hospital appointments went back to it as often as he could. His two sisters and younger brother—the former married, the latter still at medical school—were free to come and go as they wished, but the house was his now that his father, a retired surgeon, and his mother, lived in den Haag.

He had had a tiring day in Rotterdam, and the lighted windows welcomed him as he got out of the car. They were not the only welcome either—the door was opened and the dogs dashed out to greet him, the wolfhound and the Jack Russell pushing and jostling to get near their master. They all went into the house together, into the large square hall with its black and white marble floor, its plain plastered walls hung with paintings in ornate gilded frames.

They were halfway across it when they were joined by an elderly man, small and rotund, who trotted ahead of them to open double doors to one side of the hall.

The room the professor entered was large and high-ceilinged, with a great hooded fireplace on either side of which were vast sofas with a Regency mahogany centre table between them. There were two tub wing armchairs with a walnut card table between them, and a couple of Dutch mahogany and marquetry armchairs on either side of a Georgian breakfast table set between two of the long windows overlooking the grounds at the back of the house.

Against the walls there were walnut display cabinets, their shelves filled with silver and porcelain, reflecting the light from the cut-glass chandelier and the ormolu wall lights. It was a beautiful room, and magnificent; it was also lived in. There were bowls of flowers here and there, a pile of newspapers and magazines on one of the tables, a dog basket to the side of the fireplace.

The professor settled his vast frame in one of the armchairs, allowed the Jack Russell to scramble onto his knee and the wolfhound to drape himself over his feet, and poured himself a drink from the tray on the table beside him. A quiet evening, he thought with satisfaction, and, since he wasn't due anywhere until the following afternoon, a long walk with the dogs in the morning.

He was disturbed by his manservant, who came bearing letters on a salver, looking apologetic.

The professor picked them up idly. 'No phone calls, Cokker?'

'Juffrouw van Moule telephoned, to remind you that you will be dining with her family tomorrow evening.'

'Oh, Lord, I had forgotten…thank you, Cokker.'

'Anna wishes to know if half an hour is sufficient for you before dinner, *mijnheer*.'

'As soon as she likes, Cokker. It's good to be home…'

'And good to have you here,' said Cokker. They smiled at each other, for Cokker had been with the family when the professor had been born and now, a sprightly sixty-year-old, had become part and parcel of it.

The professor took the dogs for a walk after dinner, across several acres of his own grounds and into the country lane beyond. It was a chilly night, but there was a moon and stars and later there would be a frost.

He strolled along, thinking about Ermentrude. By now her father would know if he had the post he had collocated. No doubt Ermentrude would tell him all about it when he got back to St Luke's. She would give in her notice, of course, and go to Dorset with her parents and he wouldn't see her again. Which was just as well. It was, he told himself, merely a passing attraction—not even that. All he had done was to take the opportunity to improve her life.

'She will be quite happy in the country again,' he told

Solly, the wolfhound. He stooped to pick up Tip, who was getting tired, and tucked the little dog under one arm. He turned for home, dismissed Ermentrude from his mind and steered his thoughts to his future bride.

Later, lying in his great four-poster bed, Ermentrude was there again, buried beneath his thoughts and contriving to upset them.

'The girl's a nuisance,' said the professor to the empty room. 'I hope that by the time I get back to St Luke's she will be gone.'

His well-ordered life, he reflected, was being torn in shreds by a plain-faced girl who made no bones about letting him see that she had no interest in him. He slept badly and awoke in an ill humour which he had difficulty in shaking off during the day.

It was only that evening, sitting beside Anneliese at her parents' dining table, joining in the talk with the other guests, aware that Anneliese was looking particularly beautiful, that he managed to dismiss Ermentrude from his mind.

Anneliese was at her best. She knew that she looked delightful, and she exerted all her charm. She was intelligent, asking him all the right questions about his work at the hospitals he was visiting, talking knowledgeably about the health service in Holland, listening with apparent interest when he outlined the same service in England.

'Such a pity you have to go back there before Christmas. But of course you'll be back here then, won't you? Mother and I will come and stay for a while; we can discuss the wedding.'

She was clever enough not to say more than that, but went on lightly, 'Do you see any more of that funny little thing you befriended at St Luke's?'

Before he could answer, she said, 'Ruerd got involved

in a bomb explosion in London.' She addressed the table at large. 'It must have been very exciting, and there was this girl who works there whom he took home—I suppose she was in shock. I saw her when I was staying in London. So plain, my dears, and all the wrong clothes. Not at all his type. Was she, Ruerd?' She turned to smile at him.

The professor had his anger nicely in check. 'Miss Foster is a brave young lady. I think perhaps none of us know enough of her to discuss her. It is quite difficult to keep calm and do whatever it is you have to do when there's an emergency, and to keep on doing it until you're fit to drop. In such circumstances, it hardly matters whether one is plain or pretty, old or young.'

Anneliese gave a little laugh. 'Oh, Ruerd, I didn't mean to be unkind. The poor girl. And we, all sitting here in comfort talking about something we know very little about.' She touched his arm. 'Forgive me and tell us what you think of the new hospital. You were there yesterday, weren't you?'

The rest of the evening passed off pleasantly enough, but, driving himself home, the professor reflected that he hadn't enjoyed it. He had never liked Anneliese's family and friends overmuch, supposing vaguely that once they were married she would welcome his more serious friends, live the quiet life he enjoyed. He tried to imagine them married and found it impossible.

She had seemed so suitable when he'd asked her to marry him—interested in his work, anxious to meet his friends, telling him how she loved to live in the country. 'With children, of course, and dogs and horses,' she had added, and he had believed her.

Yet that very evening he had stood by, while she talked to some of her friends, and listened to her complaining sharply about the nuisance of having to visit a cousin with young children. 'They're such a bore,' she had said.

Her mother, a formidable matron who enjoyed dictating to everyone around her, had chimed in, saying, 'Children should stay in the nursery until they're fit to mix with their elders. I have always advised young girls of my acquaintance that that is the best for them. Besides, they can hamper one's life so. A good nanny is the answer.' She had smiled around at her listeners, saying, 'And I have given Anneliese the same advice, have I not, my dear?'

Her words, echoing in his head, filled him with disquiet.

Emmy meanwhile was busy. She was happy too. At least she told herself that she was several times a day. To live in the country again would be heaven—only would it be quite heaven if she was never to see the professor again? It wouldn't, but there was nothing to be done about that, and it was, after all, something she had wanted badly. Besides that, her mother and father were over the moon. She applied herself to the packing up with a cheerful energy which wasn't quite genuine, buoyed up by her mother's obvious delight.

Mr Stokes, with his rather decrepit van, and an old man and a young boy to help him, stowed the furniture tidily, leaving Emmy's bedroom intact, and a table and two chairs in the kitchen, as well as the bare necessities for living.

'It won't be for long,' said Emmy cheerfully. 'There are two lots of people coming to view the house tomorrow; I'm sure it will be sold by the time I leave.'

Her mother said anxiously, 'You will get a hot meal at the hospital, Emmy? And do keep the electric fire on while you are in the house. Empty houses are so cold.' She frowned. 'I do wonder if there might have been some other way…'

'Stop worrying, Mother. I only need a bed and some-where to have breakfast.' She didn't mention the long evenings alone and the solitary suppers. After all, it was for such a short time.

She was on night duty again, so she was there to see her mother, sitting beside Mr Stokes, leave for their new home. After they had gone she went into the kitchen and made herself some coffee. The house looked shabbier than ever now that it was almost empty, and without the animals it was so quiet. She put everything ready for an evening meal and went to bed. She was already some days into her notice. It was a satisfying thought as she dropped off. Everything was going according to plan, she thought with satisfaction.

Only she was wrong. Audrey hardly gave her time to get her coat off the following evening before bursting into furious speech.

'The nerve,' she cried. 'And there's nothing to be done about it—or so I'm told. Reorganisation, indeed, necessary amalgamation to cut expenses…'

Emmy took the envelope Audrey was offering her. 'What's the matter? What are you talking about?'

'Read it for yourself. I'm going home—and don't expect to see me tomorrow.'

She stomped away and Emmy sat down and read the letter in the envelope.

There were to be changes, she read, and regretfully her services would no longer be required. With the opening of the new hospital across the river, St Luke's and Bennett's hospitals would amalgamate and the clerical staff from Bennett's would take over various functions, of which the switchboard was one. The letter pointed out that she would be given a reference, and the likelihood of her getting a new job was high. It ended with a mealy-mouthed paragraph thanking her for her loyal services which as she had already given notice, would terminate on Friday next.

She read it through again, carefully, in case she had missed something. But it was clear enough—in two days' time she would be jobless.

She could, of course, join her mother and father. On the other hand there was far more chance of the house being sold if there was someone there to keep the estate agents on their toes and show people around. By the end of the night she had decided to say nothing to her parents. She would be able to manage on her own and she would have a week's salary, and surely an extra month's money, since she had been given barely two days' notice.

It would have been nice to have had someone to have talked things over with. The professor would have been ideal…

As it was, when the porter brought her coffee she forgot her own troubles when he told her that he was to go too. 'They've offered me a job in that new place across the river—less money, and takes me much longer to get to work. Haven't got much choice, though, have I? With a wife and baby to look after?' He glanced at her. 'What'll you do, Emmy?'

'Me? Oh, I'll be all right. Audrey was very angry…'

'You bet she was. Proper blew her top, she did. Didn't do no good. Wrongful dismissal, she said, but it seems it isn't. It's like when a firm goes bankrupt and everyone just goes home. If there's no money, see? What else is there to do?'

'Well, good luck with your job, anyway, and thanks for the coffee.'

* * *

Emmy hadn't believed Audrey when she had said that she wouldn't be there in the morning, but she had meant it. Emmy, going off duty late because a relief telephonist had had to be called in, was too tired to notice the icy rain and the leaden sky. Home, she thought, even if it is only my bedroom and a table and chairs.

Only they didn't look very welcoming when she let herself into the empty house. She boiled an egg, made toast and a pot of tea and took herself off to bed. When she had had a sleep she would mull over the turn of events and see how best to deal with it. One thing was certain: there was no way of changing it. And, being a sensible girl, she put her head on the pillow and slept.

She had time enough to think when she got up in the late afternoon. It was still raining and almost dark, and she was glad they had left the curtains hanging and some of the carpets. She showered, made tea and sat down in the kitchen to think. She would call into the estate agents on her way home in the morning and spur them on a bit. The market was slow, they had told her father, but the house was small, in fairly good order and soundly built, like all the other houses in the row. Its selling price was modest, well within the reach of anyone prudent enough to have saved a little capital and who could get a mortgage.

She allowed herself to dream a bit. There would be a little money—not much, but perhaps enough for all of them to have new clothes, perhaps have a holiday—although being in Dorset would be like a holiday itself. She would get a chance to go to a needlework school—night classes, perhaps? Start a small arts and crafts shop on her own? The possibilities were endless. She got her supper presently, and went to work for the last time.

It was a busy night, and when it was over she bade

goodbye to those she had worked with and left the hospital for the last time. She had her pay packet in her purse, and an extra month in lieu of notice, and she handed over to her older colleague, who told her that she had been working for the NHS for more than twenty years.

'I don't know what I would have done if I had been made redundant,' she said. 'I've an elderly mother and father who live with me. We make ends meet, but only just—to be out of work would have been a catastrophe.'

It was heartening to find on her way home that there had been several enquiries about the house. The agent, a weasel-faced young man she didn't much like, had arranged for them to inspect the house at any time they wished.

'You'll be there,' he told her airily. 'So it really doesn't matter when they call, if they do.'

'I can't be there all day,' Emmy told him, and was silenced by him.

'You're not on the phone—stands to reason, doesn't it? Someone will have to be there.'

'Will you ask anyone who wants to look round the house to come after one o'clock? I will stay at home for the rest of the day.'

'Suit yourself, Miss Foster. The two parties interested said they'd call in some time today.'

To go to bed was impossible; one never knew, whoever was coming might decide to buy the house. Emmy had her breakfast, tidied away the dishes and sat down on the one comfortable chair in the kitchen. Of course she went to sleep almost at once, and woke to the sound of someone thumping the door knocker and ringing the bell.

The middle-aged couple she admitted looked sour.

'Took your time, didn't you?' observed the man grumpily, and pushed past her into the hall. He and his meek-looking wife spent the next ten minutes looking round and returned to Emmy, who was waiting in the kitchen after taking them on their first survey.

'Pokey, that's what it is,' declared the man. 'You'll be lucky to sell the place at half the asking price.'

He went away, taking his wife, who hadn't said a word, with him. Emmy hadn't said anything either. There seemed to be no point in annoying the man more than necessary. There would be several more like him, she guessed.

The second couple came late in the afternoon. They made a leisurely tour and Emmy began to feel hopeful, until the woman remarked, 'It's a lot better than some we've seen. Not that we can buy a house, but it gives us some idea of what we could get if we had the money.' She smiled at Emmy. 'Nice meeting you.'

Not a very promising start, decided Emmy, locking the door behind them. Better luck tomorrow. Though perhaps people didn't come on a Saturday.

She felt more hopeful after a good night's sleep. After all, it was early days; houses didn't sell all that fast. Only it would be splendid if someone decided to buy the place before she joined her parents.

No one came. Not the next day. She had gone for a walk in the morning and then spent the rest of the day in the kitchen, listening to her small radio and knitting. Monday, she felt sure, would bring more possible buyers.

No one came, nor did they come on Tuesday, Wednesday or Thursday. She wrote a cheerful letter to her parents on Friday, did her morning's shopping and spent the rest of the day waiting for the doorbell to ring. Only it didn't.

* * *

The professor, back in London, striding into St Luke's ready for a day's work, paused on his way. While not admitting it, he was looking forward to seeing Emmy again. He hoped that all had gone according to his plan and that her father had got the job the professor's friend had found for him. Emmy would have given her notice by now. He would miss her. And a good thing that she was going, he reminded himself.

He was brought up short by the sight of the older woman sitting in Emmy's chair. He wished her a civil good morning, and asked, 'Miss Foster? Is she ill?'

'Ill? No, sir. Left. Made redundant with several others. There's been a cutting down of staff.'

He thanked her and went on his way, not unduly worried. Ermentrude would have gone to Dorset with her father and mother. He must find time to phone his friend and make sure that all had gone according to plan. She would be happy there, he reflected. And she would forget him. Only he wouldn't forget her…

He left the hospital rather earlier than usual, and on a sudden impulse, instead of going home, drove through the crowded streets and turned into the street where Emmy lived. Outside the house he stopped the car. There was a FOR SALE board fastened to the wall by the door, and the downstairs curtains were drawn across. There was a glimmer of light showing, so he got out of the car and knocked on the door.

Emmy put down the can of beans she was opening. At last here was someone come to see the house. She turned on the light in the hall and went to open the door, and, being a prudent girl, left the safety chain on. Peering round it, recognising the vast expanse of waistcoat visible, her heart did a happy little somersault.

'It is I,' said the professor impatiently, and, when she had slid back the chain, came into the narrow hall, squashing her against a wall.

Emmy wormed her way into a more dignified stance. 'Hello, sir,' she said. 'Are you back in England?' She caught his eye. 'What I mean is, I'm surprised to see you. I didn't expect to…'

He had seen the empty room and the almost bare kitchen beyond. He took her arm and bustled her into the kitchen, sat her in a chair and said, 'Tell me why you are here alone in an empty house. Your parents?'

'Well, it's a long story…'

'I have plenty of time,' he told her. 'And I am listening.'

CHAPTER FIVE

EMMY told him without embellishments. 'So you see it's all turned out marvellously. We just have to sell this house—that's why I'm here. We thought I'd have to give a month's notice, and it seemed a splendid idea for me to stay on until I could leave and try and sell the house at the same time. Only being made redundant was a surprise. I've not told Father, of course.'

'You are here alone, with no furniture, no comforts?'

'Oh, I've got my bed upstairs, and a cupboard, and I don't need much. Of course, we thought I'd be at the hospital all day or all night. Actually,' she told him, wanting to put a good light on things, 'It's worked out very well, for I stay at home each day from one o'clock so that I can show people round...'

'You get many prospective buyers?'

'Well, not many, not every day. It isn't a very attractive house.'

The professor agreed silently to this. 'You will join your parents for Christmas? Have you a job in mind to go to?'

'Yes. Well, I've hardly had time, have I?' she asked reasonably. Then added, 'Perhaps I'll be able to take a course in embroidery and needlework...'

She didn't go on; he didn't want to know her plans. She asked instead, 'Did you have a pleasant time in Holland?'

'Yes. I'll wait here while you put a few things into a bag, Ermentrude. You will come back with me.'

'Indeed, I won't. Whatever next? I'm quite all right here, thank you. Besides, I must be here to show people round.' She added on a sudden thought, 'Whatever would your fiancée think? I mean, she's not to know that we don't like each other.' Emmy went bright pink. 'I haven't put that very well…'

'No, you haven't. You have, however, made it quite plain that you do not need my help.'

The professor got to his feet. He said coldly, 'Goodbye, Ermentrude.' And, while she was still searching for the right reply, let himself out of the house.

Emmy listened to the car going away down the street; she made almost no sound. She sat where she was for quite some time, doing her best not to cry.

Presently she got up and got her supper, and since there was nothing to do she went to bed.

She wasn't sure what woke her up. She sat up in bed, listening; the walls were thin, it could have been Mr Grant or Mrs Grimes dropping something or banging a door. She lay down again and then shot up once more. The noise, a stealthy shuffling, was downstairs.

She didn't give herself time to feel frightened. She got out of bed quietly, put on her dressing gown and slippers and, seizing the only weapon handy—her father's umbrella which had somehow got left behind—she opened her door and peered out onto the landing. Someone was there, someone with a torch, and they had left the front door open too.

The nerve, reflected Emmy, in a rage, and swept downstairs, switching on the landing light as she did so. The man was in the empty sitting room, but he came out fast and reached the hall. He was young, his face half hidden by a scarf, a cap pulled down over his eyes and, after his first shock, he gave a nasty little laugh.

'Cor, lummy— An empty 'ouse an' a girl. Alone, are you? Well, let's 'ave yer purse, and make it quick.'

Emmy poked him with the umbrella. 'You get out of this house and you make it quick,' she told him. She gave him another prod. 'Go on…'

He made to take the umbrella from her, but this time she whacked him smartly over the head so that he howled with pain.

'Out,' said Emmy in a loud voice which she hoped hid her fright. She switched on the hall light now, hoping that someone, even at two o'clock in the morning, would see it. But the man, she was glad to see, had retreated to the door. She followed him, umbrella at the ready, and he walked backwards into the street.

Rather puffed up with her success at getting rid of him, she followed him, unaware that the man's mate was standing beside the door, out of sight. She heard him call out before something hard hit her on the head and she keeled over.

She didn't hear them running away since for the moment she had been knocked out. But Mr Grant, trotting to the window to see why there was a light shining into the street, saw them. Old though he was, he made his way downstairs and out of his house to where Emmy lay. Emmy didn't answer when he spoke to her, and she was very pale. He crossed the road and rang the bell of the house opposite. It sounded very loud at that time of the night. He rang again, and presently a window was opened and the teenager hung his head out.

'Come down, oh, do come down—Ermentrude has been hurt.'

The head disappeared and a moment later the boy, in his coat and boots, came out. 'Thieves? Take anything, did they? Not that there's anything to take.' He bent over Emmy. 'I'll get her inside and the door shut.'

He was a big lad, and strong; he picked Emmy up and carried her into the kitchen and set her in a chair. 'Put the kettle on,' he suggested. 'I'll be back in a tick; I'll get my phone.'

As he came back into the kitchen Emmy opened her eyes. She said crossly, 'I've got the most awful headache. Someone hit me.'

'You're right there. Who shall I ring? You'd better have a doctor—and the police.' He stood looking at her for a moment, and was joined by Mr Grant. 'You can't stay here, that's for certain. Got any friends? Someone to look after you?'

Mr Grant had brought her a wet towel, and she was holding it to her head. She felt sick and frightened and there was no one… Yes, there was. He might not like her, but he would help and she remembered his number; she had rung it time and again from the hospital.

She said muzzily, 'Yes, there's someone, if you'd tell him. Ask him if he would come.' She gave the boy the number and closed her eyes.

'He'll be along in fifteen minutes,' said the boy. 'Lucky the streets are empty at this time of night. Did they take anything?'

Emmy shook her head, and then wished she hadn't. 'No. There's nothing to take; my purse and bag are upstairs and they didn't get that far.' She said tiredly, 'Thank you both for coming to help me; I'm very grateful.'

As far as she was concerned, she thought, they can

make all the noise they like and I'll never even think of complaining.

Mr Grant gave her a cup of tea and she tried to drink it, holding it with both shaky hands while the boy phoned the police. Then there was nothing to do but wait. The boy and Mr Grant stood drinking tea, looking rather helplessly at her.

'I'm going to be sick,' said Emmy suddenly, and lurched to the sink.

Which was how the professor found her a couple of minutes later.

The boy had let him in. 'You the bloke she told me to phone?' he asked suspiciously.

'Yes. I'm a doctor. Have you called the police?'

'Yes. She's in the kitchen being sick.'

Emmy was past caring about anyone or anything. When she felt the professor's large, cool hand on her wrist, she mumbled, 'I knew you'd come. I feel sick, and I've got a headache.'

He opened his bag. 'I'm not surprised; you have a bump the size of a hen's egg on your head.' His hands were very gentle. 'Keep still, Ermentrude, while I take a look.'

She hardly felt his hands after that, and while he dealt with the lump and the faint bleeding he asked what had happened.

Mr Grant and the boy both told him at once, talking together.

'The police?'

'They said they were on their way.'

The professor said gravely, 'It is largely due to the quick thinking and courage of both of you that Ermentrude isn't more severely injured. I'll get her to hospital just as soon as the police get here.'

They came a few minutes later, took statements from Mr Grant and the boy, agreed with the professor that Ermentrude wasn't in a fit state to say anything at the moment and agreed to interview her later. 'We will lock the door and keep the key at the station.' The officer swept his gaze round the bare room. 'No one lives here?'

'Yes, me,' said Ermentrude. 'Just for a few weeks—until someone wants to buy it. Do you want me to explain?' She opened her eyes and closed them again.

'Wait until you know what you're talking about,' advised the professor bracingly. He spoke to one of the officers. 'Miss Foster is staying here for a short time; her parents have moved and she has stayed behind to settle things up.' He added, 'You will want to see her, of course. She will be staying at my house.' He gave the address, heedless of Emmy's mutterings.

'Now, if I might have a blanket in which to wrap her, I'll take her straight to St Luke's. I'm a consultant there. She needs to be X-rayed.'

Emmy heard this in a muzzy fashion. It wouldn't do at all; she must say something. She lifted her head too quickly, and then bent it over the sink just in time. The professor held her head in a matter-of-fact way while the others averted their gaze.

'The blanket?' asked the professor again, and the boy went upstairs and came back with her handbag and the quilt from Emmy's bed. The professor cleaned her up in a businesslike manner, wrapped her in the quilt and picked her up.

'If I'm not at my home I'll be at the hospital.' He thanked Mr Grant and the boy, bade the officers a civil goodnight, propped Emmy in the back of the car and, when she began to mumble a protest, told her to be quiet.

He said it in a very gentle voice, though. She closed her eyes, lying back in the comfortable seat, and tried to forget her raging headache.

At the hospital she was whisked straight to X-Ray. She was vaguely aware of the radiographer complaining good-naturedly to the professor and of lying on a trolley for what seemed hours.

'No harm done,' said the professor quietly in her ear. 'I'm going to see to that lump, and then you can be put to bed and sleep.'

She was wheeled to Casualty then, and lay quietly while he bent over her, peering into her eyes, putting a dressing on her head. She was drowsy now, but his quiet voice mingling with Sister's brisk tone was soothing. She really didn't care what happened next.

When he lifted her into the car once more, she said, 'Not here…' But since the professor took no notice of her she closed her eyes again. She had been given a pill to swallow in Casualty; her headache was almost bearable and she felt nicely sleepy.

Beaker was waiting when the professor reached his house, carried Emmy indoors and asked, 'You got Mrs Burge to come round? I had no time to give you details. If I carry Miss Foster upstairs perhaps she will help her to bed.'

'She's upstairs waiting, sir. What a to-do. The poor young lady—knocked out, was she?'

'Yes. I'll tell you presently, Beaker. I could do with a drink, and I expect you could, too. Did Mrs Burge make any objections?'

'Not her! I fetched her like you told me to, and she'll stay as long as she's wanted.'

The professor was going upstairs with Emmy, fast asleep now, in his arms. 'Splendid.'

Mrs Burge met him on the small landing. 'In the small guest room, sir. Just you lay her down on the bed and I'll make her comfortable.'

She was a tall, bony woman with hair screwed into an old-fashioned bun and a sharp nose. A widow, she had been coming each day to help Beaker for some time now, having let it be known from the outset that through no fault of her own she had fallen on hard times and needed to earn her living.

Beaker got on well with her, and she had developed an admiration for the professor, so that being routed out of her bed in the early hours of the morning was something she bore with equanimity. She said now, 'Just you leave the young lady to me, sir, and go and have a nap—you'll be dead on your feet and a day's work ahead of you.'

The professor said, 'Yes, Mrs Burge,' in a meek voice, merely adding that he would be up presently just to make sure that Emmy's pulse was steady and that she slept still. 'I know I leave her in good hands,' he told Mrs Burge, and she bridled with pleasure.

For all her somewhat forbidding appearance she was a kind-hearted woman. She tucked Emmy, still sleeping, into bed, dimmed the bedside light and sat down in the comfortable armchair, keeping faithful watch.

'She's not moved,' she told the professor presently. 'Sleeping like a baby.'

He bent over the bed, took Emmy's pulse and felt her head.

'I'll leave these pills for her to take, Mrs Burge. See that she has plenty to drink, and if she wants to eat, so much the better. A couple of days in bed and she'll be quite herself. There's only the mildest of concussions, and the cut will heal quickly.

'I'm going to the hospital in an hour or so and shall be there all day. Ring me if you're worried. Beaker will give you all the assistance you require, and once Ermentrude is

awake there is no reason why you shouldn't leave her from
time to time. I'll be back presently when I've had breakfast so that you can have yours with Beaker.'

He went away to shower and dress and eat his breakfast
and then returned, and Mrs Burge went downstairs to
where Beaker was waiting with eggs and bacon.

Emmy hadn't stirred; the professor sat down in a chair,
watching her. She suited the room, he decided—quite a
small room, but charming with its white furniture, its walls
covered with a delicate paper of pale pink roses and soft
green leaves. The curtains were white, and the bedspread
matched the wallpaper exactly. It was a room he had
planned with the help of his younger sister, whose small
daughter slept in it when they visited him.

'Though once you're married, Ruerd,' she had told him
laughingly, 'you'll need it for your own daughter.'

Emmy, with her hair all over the pillow, looked very
young and not at all plain, he decided. When Mrs Burge came
back he said a word or two to her, bent over the bed once
more and stopped himself just in time from kissing Emmy.

It was late in the morning when Emmy woke, to stare up
into Mrs Burge's face. She was on the point of asking
'Where am I?' and remembered that only heroines in books
said that. Instead she said, 'I feel perfectly all right; I
should like to get up.'

'Not just yet, love. I'm going to bring you a nice little pot
of tea and something tasty to eat. You're to sit up a bit if you
feel like it. I'll put another pillow behind you. There…'

'I don't remember very clearly,' began Emmy. 'I was
taken to the hospital and I went to sleep.'

'Why, you're snug and safe here in Professor ter
Mennolt's house, dearie, and me and Beaker are keeping

an eye on you. He's gone to the hospital, but he'll be home this evening.'

Emmy sat up too suddenly and winced. 'I can't stay here. There's no one at the house—the estate agent won't know—someone might want to buy it...'

'Leave everything to the professor, ducks. You may be sure he'll have thought of what's to be done.'

Mrs Burge went away and came back presently with a tray daintily laid with fine china—a teapot, cup and saucer, milk and sugar. 'Drink this, there's a good girl,' she said. 'Beaker's getting you a nice little lunch and then you must have another nap.'

'I'm quite able to get up,' said Emmy, to Mrs Burge's departing back.

'You'll stay just where you are until I say you may get out of bed,' said the professor from the door. 'Feeling better?'

'Yes, thank you. I'm sorry I've given you all so much trouble. Couldn't I have stayed in hospital and then gone home?'

'No,' said the professor. 'You will stay here today and tomorrow, and then we will decide what is to be done. I have phoned the estate agent. He has a set of keys for your house and will deal with anyone who wishes to view it. The police will come some time this afternoon to ask you a few questions if you feel up to it.'

'You're very kind, sir, and I'm grateful. I'll be quite well by tomorrow, I can go...'

'Where?' He was leaning over the foot of the bed, watching her.

She took a sip of tea. 'I'm sure Mrs Grimes would put me up.'

'Mrs Grimes—the lady with the powerful voice? Don't talk nonsense, Ermentrude.' He glanced up as Mrs Burge came in with a tray. 'Here is your lunch; eat all of it and drink all the lemonade in that jug. I'll be back this evening.'

He went away and presently out of the house, for he had a clinic that early afternoon. He had missed lunch in order to see Ermentrude, and had only time to swallow a cup of coffee before his first patient arrived.

Emmy ate her lunch under Mrs Burge's watchful eye and, rather to her surprise, went to sleep again to wake and find another tray of tea, and Mrs Burge shaking out a gossamer-fine nightie.

'If you feel up to it, I'm to help you have a bath, love. You're to borrow one of the professor's sister's nighties. You'll feel a whole lot better.'

'Would someone be able to fetch my clothes so that I can go home tomorrow?' asked Emmy.

'Beaker will run me over this evening. You just tell me what you want and I'll pack it up for you. Professor ter Mennolt's got the keys.'

'Oh, thank you. You're very kind. Were you here when I came last night?'

'Yes—Beaker fetched me—three o'clock in the morning…'

'You must be so tired. I'm quite all right, Mrs Burge. Can't you go home and have a good sleep?'

'Bless you, ducks, I'm as right as a trivet; don't you worry your head about me. Now, how about a bath?'

Getting carefully out of bed, Emmy discovered that she still had a headache and for the moment wished very much to crawl back between the sheets. But the thought of being seen in her present neglected state got her onto her feet and into the adjoining bathroom, and once in the warm, scented water with Mrs Burge sponging her gently she began to feel better.

'I suppose I can't wash my hair?'

'Lawks, no, love. I'll give it a bit of a comb, but I daren't go messing about with it until the professor says so.'

'It's only a small cut,' said Emmy, anxious to look her best.

'And a lump the size of an egg—that'll take a day or two. A proper crack on the head and no mistake. Lucky that neighbour saw the light and the men running away. It could have been a lot worse,' said Mrs Burge with a gloomy relish.

Emmy, dried, powdered and in the kind of nightgown she had often dreamed of possessing, sat carefully in a chair while Mrs Burge made her bed and shook up her pillows. Once more settled against them, Emmy sighed with relief. It was absurd that a bang on the head should make her feel so tired. She closed her eyes and went to sleep.

Which was how the professor found her when he got home. He stood looking down at her for a long minute, and in turn was watched by Mrs Burge.

They went out of the room together. 'Go home, Mrs Burge,' he told her. 'You've been more than kind. If you could come in tomorrow, I would be most grateful. I must contrive to get Ermentrude down to her parents—they are in Dorset and know nothing of this. They are moving house, and I don't wish to make things more difficult for them than I must. Another day of quiet rest here and I think I might drive her down on the following day…'

Mrs Burge crossed her arms across her thin chest. 'Begging your pardon, sir, but I'll be back here to sleep tonight.'

He didn't smile, but said gravely, 'That would be good of you, Mrs Burge, as long as you find that convenient.'

'It's convenient.' She nodded. 'And I'll make sure the young lady's all right tomorrow.'

'I'm in your debt, Mrs Burge. Come back when you like this evening. Is there a room ready for you?'

'Yes, sir, I saw to that myself.' She hesitated. 'Miss Ermentrude did ask if someone could fetch her clothes. I said I'd go this evening…'

'Tell me when you want to go; I'll drive you over. Perhaps you had better ask her if she needs anything else. Money or papers of any sort.'

Emmy woke presently and, feeling much better, made a list of what she needed and gave it to Mrs Burge.

'I'm off home for a bit,' said that lady. 'But I'll be back this evening. Beaker will bring you up some supper presently. You just lie there like a good girl.'

So Emmy lay back and, despite a slight headache, tried to make plans. Once she had been pronounced fit, she decided, she would go back to the house. She didn't much fancy being there alone, but reassured herself with the thought that lightning never struck twice in the same place… She would go to the estate agents again, too, and there was only another week or so until Christmas now.

Her thoughts were interrupted by the professor and her supper tray.

He greeted her with an impersonal hello. 'Beaker has done his best, so be sure and eat everything.'

He put the tray down, set the bed table across her knees and plumped up her pillows. 'I think you might get up tomorrow—potter round the house, go into the garden— well wrapped-up. I'll take you home the day after.'

'You're very kind, but I must go back to the house, just in case someone wants to buy it. I mean, I can't afford to miss a chance. It'll have to be left empty when I go home at Christmas, and you know how awful houses look when they're empty. So if you don't mind…'

'I do mind, Ermentrude, and you'll do as I say. I'll phone the estate agent if it will set your mind at rest and rearrange things. Do you want me to tell your parents what has happened?'

'Oh, no—they're getting the house straight, and Father's at the school all day so it's taking a bit of time. They've enough to worry about. They don't need to know anyway.'

'Just as you wish. Does Mrs Burge know what to fetch for you?'

'Yes, thank you. I gave her a list. I've only a few clothes there; Mother took the rest with her.'

'Then I'll say goodnight, Ermentrude. Sleep well.'

She was left to eat her supper, a delicious meal Beaker had devised with a good deal of thought. It was he who came to get the tray later, bringing with him fresh lemonade and a fragile china plate with mouth-watering biscuits.

'I make them myself, miss,' he told her, beaming at her praise of the supper. 'Mrs Burge will look in on you when she gets back, with a nice drop of hot milk.'

'Thank you, Beaker, you have been so kind and I'm giving you a lot of extra work.'

'A pleasure, miss.'

'I heard Charlie barking…'

'A spirited dog, miss, and a pleasure to have in the house. Humphrey and he are quite partial to each other. When you come downstairs tomorrow he will be delighted to see you.'

Emmy, left alone, ate some of the biscuits, drank some of the lemonade and thought about the professor. His household ran on oiled wheels, that was obvious. His Anneliese, when she married him, would have very little to do—a little tasteful flower-arranging perhaps, occasional shopping, although she thought that Beaker might not like that. And of course later there would be the children to look after.

Emmy frowned. She tried to imagine Anneliese nursing a baby, changing nappies or coping with a toddler and failed. She gave up thinking about it and thought about the professor instead, wishing he would come home again and come and see her. She liked him, she decided, even though he was difficult to get to know. Then, why should he wish her to know too much about him? She had no place in his life.

Much later she heard the front door close, and Charlie barking. He and Mrs Burge went home. She lay, watching the door. When it opened Mrs Burge came in, a suitcase in one hand, a glass of milk in the other.

'Still awake? I've brought everything you asked for, and Professor ter Mennolt went to see the estate agent at his home and fixed things up. No one's been to look at the house.' Mrs Burge's sniff implied that she wasn't surprised at that. 'We looked everywhere to make sure that things were just so. And there's some post. Would you like to read it now?'

She put the milk on the bedside table. 'Drink your milk first. It's time you were sleeping.'

Emmy asked hesitantly, 'Are you going home now, Mrs Burge?'

'No, ducks. I'll be here, just across the landing, if you want me. Now I'll just hang up your things…'

Emmy stifled disappointment. There was no reason why the professor should wish to see her. He must, in fact, be heartily sick of her by now, disrupting his life.

The professor was talking on the phone. Presently he got his coat, ushered Charlie into the back of the car and, with a word to Beaker, drove himself to St Luke's where one of his patients was giving rise to anxiety.

He got home an hour later, ate the dinner which Beaker served him with the air of someone who had long learned not to mind when his carefully prepared meals were eaten hours after they should have been, and went to his study to work at his desk with the faithful Charlie sprawled over his feet.

Waking the following morning, Emmy decided that she felt perfectly well again. She ate her breakfast in bed, since Mrs Burge told her sternly not to get up till later.

'Professor ter Mennolt went off an hour ago,' she told Emmy. 'What a life that man leads, never an hour to call his own.'

Which wasn't quite true, but Emmy knew what she meant. 'I suppose all doctors are at everyone's beck and call, but it must be a rewarding life.'

'Well, let's hope he gets his reward; he deserves it,' said Mrs Burge. 'Time that fiancée of his made up her mind to marry him.' She sniffed. 'Wants too much, if you ask me. Doesn't like this house—too small, she says…'

'Too small?' Emmy put down her cup. 'But it's a big house—I mean, big enough for a family.'

'Huh,' said Mrs Burge forcefully. 'Never mind a family, she likes to entertain—dinner parties and friends visiting. She doesn't much like Beaker, either.'

Emmy, aware that she shouldn't be gossiping, nonetheless asked, 'But why not? He's the nicest person…'

'True enough, love. Looks after the professor a treat.'

'So do you, Mrs Burge.'

'Me? I come in each day to give a hand, like. Been doing it for years, ever since the professor bought the house. A very nice home he's made of it, too. I have heard that he's got a tip-top place in Holland, too. Well, it stands to reason, doesn't it? He's over there for the best part of the year—only comes here for a month or two, though he pops over if he's needed. Much in demand, he is.'

She picked up Emmy's tray. 'Now, you have a nice bath and get dressed and come downstairs when you're ready. I'll be around and just you call if you want me. We'd better pack your things later on; the professor's driving you home in the morning.'

So Emmy got herself out of bed, first taking a look at her lump before going to the bathroom. The swelling had almost gone and the cut was healing nicely. She stared at her reflection for several moments; she looked a fright, and she was going to wash her hair before anyone told her not to.

Bathed, and with her hair in a damp plait, she went downstairs to find Beaker hovering in the hall.

His, 'Good morning, miss,' was affable. 'There's a cup of coffee in the small sitting room; it's nice and cosy there.'

He led the way and opened a door onto a quite small room at the back of the house. It was furnished very comfortably, and there was a fire burning in the elegant fireplace. A small armchair had been drawn up to it, flanked by a table on which were newspapers and a magazine or two. Sitting in front of the fire, waving his tail, asking to be noticed, was Charlie.

Emmy, sitting down, could think of nothing more delightful than to be the owner of such a room and such a dog, with a faithful old friend like Beaker smoothing out life's wrinkles. She said on a happy sigh, 'This is such a lovely house, Beaker, and everything is so beautifully polished and cared for.'

Beaker allowed himself to smile. 'The master and I, we're happy here, or so I hope, miss.' He went, soft-footed, to the door. 'I'll leave you to drink your coffee; lunch will be at one o'clock.'

He opened the door and she could hear Mrs Burge Hoovering somewhere.

'I suppose the professor won't be home for lunch?'

'No, miss. Late afternoon. He has an evening engagement.'

She put on her coat and went into the garden with Charlie after lunch. For one belonging to a town house the garden was surprisingly large, and cleverly planned to make the most of its space. She wandered up and down while Charlie pottered, and presently when they went indoors she sought out Beaker.

'Do you suppose I might take Charlie for a walk?' she asked him.

Beaker looked disapproving. 'I don't think the professor would care for that, miss. Charlie has had a long walk, early this morning with his master. He will go out again when the professor comes home. There's a nice fire burning in the drawing room. Mrs Burge asked me to let you know that she'll be back this evening if you should need any help with your packing. I understand that you are to make an early start.'

So Emmy retreated to the drawing room and curled up by the fire with Charlie beside her and Humphrey on her lap. She leafed through the newspapers and magazines on the table beside her, not reading them, her mind busy with her future. Christmas was too close for her to look for work; she would stay at home and help to get their new house to rights. There would be curtains to sew and hang, possessions to be stowed away in cupboards.

She wondered what the house was like. Her mother had written to tell her that it was delightful, but had had no time to describe it. There had been a slight hitch, she had written; the previous occupant's furniture was for the most part still in the house owing to some delay in its transport. 'But,' her mother had written, 'we shall be quite settled in by the time you come.'

Beaker brought tea presently; tiny sandwiches, fairy cakes and a chocolate cake which he assured her he had baked especially for her. 'Most young ladies enjoy them,' he told her.

Emmy was swallowing the last morsel when Charlie bounded to his feet, barking, and a moment later the professor came into the room.

His 'Hello,' was friendly and casual. He sat down, then enquired how she felt and cut himself a slice of cake.

'I'll run you home in the morning,' he told her. 'The day after tomorrow I shall be going to Holland.'

'There's no need,' said Emmy.

'Don't be silly,' said the professor at his most bracing. 'You can't go back to an empty house, and in a very short time you would be going home anyway. There seems little chance of selling the house at the moment; I phoned the agent this morning. There's nothing of value left there, is there?'

She shook her head. 'No, only my bed and the bed-clothes and a few bits of furniture.'

'There you are, then. We'll leave at eight o'clock.' He got up. 'Charlie and I are going for our walk—I shall be out tonight. Beaker's looking after you?'

'Oh, yes, thank you.'

'Mrs Burge will come again this evening. Ask for anything you want.'

His smile was remote as he went away.

She was still sitting there when he returned an hour later with Charlie, but he didn't come into the drawing room, and later still she heard him leave the house once more. Beaker, opening the door for Charlie to come in, said that Mrs Burge was in the kitchen if she needed her for anything. 'I'll be serving dinner in half an hour, Miss. May I pour you a glass of sherry?'

It might lift her unexpected gloom, thought Emmy, accepting. Why she should feel so downcast she had no idea; she should have been on the top of the world—leaving London and that pokey house and going to live miles away in Dorset. She wouldn't miss anything or anyone, she told herself, and the professor, for one, would be glad to see her go; she had caused enough disruption in his life.

Beaker had taken great pains with dinner—mushroom soup, sole *à la femme*, creamed potatoes and baby sprouts, and an apricot pavlova to follow these. He poured her a glass of wine too, murmuring that the professor had told him to do so.

She drank her coffee in Humphrey's company and then, since she was heartily sick of her own company, went in search of Mrs Burge. There was still some packing to do, and that lady came willingly enough to give her help, even though it wasn't necessary. It passed an hour or so in comfortable chat and presently Emmy said that she would go to bed.

'We're to go early in the morning, so I'll say goodbye, Mrs Burge, and thank you for being so kind and helpful.'

'Bless you, ducks, it's been a pleasure, and I'll be up to see you off. Beaker will have breakfast on the table sharp at half past seven—I'll give you a call at seven, shall I?'

She turned on her way out. 'I must say you look a sight better than when you got here.'

Emmy, alone, went to the triple looking-glass on the dressing table and took a good look. If she was looking better now she must have looked a perfect fright before.

No wonder the professor showed little interest in her company. Anyway, she reminded herself, his mind would be on Anneliese.

She woke in the morning to find her bedside lamp on and Mrs Burge standing there with a tray of tea.

'It's a nasty old day,' said Mrs Burge. 'Still dark, too. You've got half an hour. The professor's already up and out with Charlie.'

The thought of keeping him waiting spurred Emmy on to dress with speed. She was downstairs with only moments to spare as he and Charlie came into the house.

His good morning was spoken warmly. He's glad I'm going, thought Emmy as she answered cheerfully.

'There's still time to put me on a train,' she told him as they sat down to breakfast. 'It would save you a miserable drive.'

He didn't bother to answer. 'The roads will be pretty empty for another hour or so,' he observed, just as though she hadn't spoken. 'We should get to Littleton Mangate by mid-morning. Ready to leave, are you?'

Emmy went to thank Beaker and Mrs Burge, and got into her coat while Beaker fetched her case down to the car. It was bitterly cold, and she took a few quick breaths before she got into the car, glad to see Charlie already sprawling on the back seat. It was almost like having a third person in the car, even though he obviously intended to go to sleep.

It was striking eight o'clock as they drove away, starting the tedious first part of their journey through London's streets and presently the suburbs.

CHAPTER SIX

IT WAS still quite dark, and the rain was turning to sleet. The professor didn't speak and Emmy made no attempt to talk. In any case she couldn't think of anything to say. The weather, that useful topic of conversation, was hardly conducive to small talk, and he had never struck her as a man who enjoyed talking for the sake of it. She stared out of the window and watched the city streets gradually give way to rows of semi-detached houses with neat front gardens, and these in turn recede to be replaced by larger houses set in their own gardens and then, at last, open country and the motorway.

Beyond asking her if she was warm enough and comfortable, the professor remained silent. Emmy sat back in her comfortable seat and thought about her future. She had thought about it rather a lot in the last few days, largely because she didn't want to think too much about the past few weeks.

She was going to miss the professor, she admitted to herself. She wouldn't see him again after today, but she hoped that he would be happy with Anneliese. He had annoyed her on several occasions, but he was a good man and kind—the sort of kindness which was practical, and if he sometimes spoke his mind rather too frankly she supposed he was entitled to do so.

As the motorway merged into the A303 he turned the car into the service station. 'Coffee? We've made good time. You go on in; I'll take Charlie for a quick trot. I'll see you in the café.'

The place was full, which made their lack of conversation easier to bear. Emmy, painstakingly making small talk and receiving nothing but brief, polite replies, presently gave up. On a wave of ill humour she said, 'Well, if you don't want to talk, we won't.' She added hastily, going red in the face, 'I'm sorry, that was rude. I expect you have a lot to think about.'

He looked at her thoughtfully. 'Yes, Ermentrude, I have. And, strangely, in your company I do not feel compelled to keep up a flow of chat.'

'That's all right, then.' She smiled at him, for it seemed to her that he had paid her a compliment.

They drove on presently through worsening weather. All the same her heart lifted at the sight of open fields and small villages. Nearing their journey's end, the professor turned off the A303 and took a narrow cross-country road, and Emmy said, 'You know the way? You've been here before?'

'No.' He turned to smile at her. 'I looked at the map. We're almost there.'

Shortly after that they went through a village and turned off into a lane overhung with bare winter trees. Round a corner, within their view, was Emmy's new house.

The professor brought the car to a halt, and after a moment's silence Emmy said, 'Oh, this can't be it,' although she knew that it was. The lodge itself was charming, even on a winter's day, but its charm was completely obliterated by the conglomeration of things around it, leaving it half-buried. Her father's car stood at the open gate, for the garage was overflowing with furniture. There was more furniture stacked and covered by tarpaulins in heaps in front of the house, a van parked on the small lawn to one side of the lodge and a stack of pipes under a hedge.

'Oh, whatever has happened?' asked Emmy. 'Surely Father hasn't…'

The professor put a large hand on hers. 'Supposing we go and have a look?'

He got out of the car and went to open her door and then let Charlie out, and together they went up the narrow path to the house.

It wasn't locked. Emmy opened it and called, 'Mother?'

They heard Mrs Foster's surprised voice from somewhere in the house and a moment later she came into the tiny hall.

'Darling—Emmy, how lovely to see you. We didn't expect you…' She looked at the professor. 'Is everything all right?'

He shook hands. 'I think it is we who should be asking you that, Mrs Foster.'

Mrs Foster had an arm round Emmy. 'Come into the kitchen; it's the only room that's comfortable. We hoped to be settled in by the time you came, Emmy. There's been a hitch…'

She led them to the kitchen with Charlie at their heels. 'Sit down; I'll make us some coffee.'

The kitchen wasn't quite warm enough, but it was furnished with a table and chairs, and there were two easy chairs at each side of the small Aga. China and crockery, knives and forks, spoons and mugs and glasses were arranged on a built-in dresser and there was a pretty latticed window over the sink.

Mrs Foster waved a hand. 'Of course all this is temporary; in a week or two we shall be settled in.'

'Mother, what has happened?' Emmy sat down at the table. Enoch and Snoodles had jumped onto her lap while George investigated Charlie.

The professor was still standing, leaning against the wall, silent. Only when Mrs Foster handed round the coffee mugs and sat down did he take a chair.

'So unfortunate,' said Mrs Foster. 'Mr Bennett, whom your father replaced, died suddenly the very day I moved down here. His furniture was to have been taken to his sister's house where he intended to live, but, of course, she didn't want it, and anyway he had willed it to a nephew who lives somewhere in the north of England. He intends to come and decide what to do with it, but he's put it off twice already and says there's no need for it to be put in store as he'll deal with it when he comes. Only he doesn't come and here we are, half in and half out as it were.'

She drank from her mug. 'Your father is extremely happy here, and since he's away for most of the day we manage very well. School breaks up tomorrow, so he will be free after that. We didn't tell you, Emmy, because we hoped—still do hope—that Mr Bennett's nephew will do something about the furniture.'

'Whose van is that outside?' asked Emmy.

'The plumber, dear. There's something wrong with the boiler—he says he'll have it right in a day or two.' Mrs Foster looked worried. 'I'm so sorry we weren't ready for you, but we'll manage. You may have to sleep on the sofa; it's in the sitting room.' She looked doubtful. 'There's furniture all over the place, I'm afraid, but we can clear a space…'

She looked at Emmy. 'I don't suppose the house is sold, Emmy?'

'No, Mother, but there have been several people to look at it. The agent's got the keys…'

'We didn't expect you just yet.' Her mother looked enquiring. 'Has something gone wrong?'

'I'll tell you later,' said Emmy. She turned to the professor, who still hadn't uttered a word. 'It was very kind of you to bring me here,' she said. 'I hope it hasn't upset your day too much.'

'Should I be told something?' asked her mother.

'Later, Mother,' said Emmy quickly. 'I'm sure Professor ter Mennolt wants to get back to London as quickly as possible.'

The professor allowed himself a small smile. He said quietly, 'There is a great deal you should be told, Mrs Foster, and if I may I'll tell it, for I can see that Ermentrude won't say a word until I'm out of the way.'

'Emmy's been ill,' said Mrs Foster in a motherly panic.

'Allow me to explain.' And, when Emmy opened her mouth to speak, he said, 'No, Ermentrude, do not interrupt me.'

He explained. His account of Emmy's misfortunes was succinct, even dry. He sounded, thought Emmy, listening to his calm voice, as if he were dictating a diagnosis, explaining something to a sister on a ward round.

When he had finished, Mrs Foster said, 'We are deeply grateful to you—my husband and I. I don't know how we can thank you enough for taking such care of Emmy.'

'A pleasure,' said the professor in a noncommittal voice which made Emmy frown. Of course it hadn't been a pleasure; she had been a nuisance. She hoped that he would go now so that she need never see him again. The thought gave her such a pang of unhappiness that she went quite pale.

He had no intention of going. He accepted Mrs Foster's

invitation to share the snack lunch she was preparing, and remarked that he would like to have a talk with Mr Foster.

'He comes home for lunch?' he enquired blandly.

'Well, no. He has it at school, but he's got a free hour at two o'clock; he told me this morning.'

'Splendid. If I may, I'll walk up to the school and have a chat.'

Emmy was on the point of asking what about when he caught her eye.

'No, Ermentrude, don't ask!' The animals had settled before the stove. The professor got up. 'I'll bring in your things, Ermentrude.'

He sounded impersonal and nonchalant, but something stopped her from asking the questions hovering on her tongue. Why should he want to talk to her father? she wondered.

They had their lunch presently—tinned soup and toasted cheese—sitting round the kitchen table, and Mrs Foster and the professor were never at a loss for conversation. Emmy thought of the silent journey they had just made and wondered what it was that kept him silent in her company. It was a relief when he got into his coat again and started on the five-minute walk to the school.

Mr Foster, if he was surprised to see the professor, didn't say so. He led the way to a small room near the classrooms, remarking that they would be undisturbed there.

'You want to see me, Professor?' He gave him a sharp glance. 'Is this to do with Emmy? She isn't ill? You say she is with her mother…'

'No, no. She has had a mild concussion and a nasty cut on the head, but, if you will allow me, I will explain…'

Which he did in the same dry manner which he had employed at the lodge. Only this time he added rather more detail.

'I am deeply indebted to you,' said Mr Foster. 'Emmy didn't say a word—if she had done so my wife would have returned to London immediately.

'Of course. Ermentrude was determined that you should know nothing about it. It was unfortunate that she should have been made redundant with such short notice, although I believe she wasn't unduly put out about that. I had no idea that she was alone in the house until I returned to London.'

Mr Foster gave him a thoughtful look and wondered why the professor should sound concerned, but he said nothing. 'Well, once we have got this business of the furniture and the plumbing settled, we shall be able to settle down nicely. I'm sure that Emmy will find a job, and in the meantime there's plenty for her to do at home.'

'Unfortunate that Christmas is so close,' observed the professor. 'Is it likely that you will be settled in by then?'

Mr Foster frowned. 'Unfortunately, no. I had a phone message this morning—this nephew is unable to deal with the removal of Mr Bennett's furniture until after Christmas. He suggests that it stays where it is for the moment. I suppose we shall be able to manage...'

'Well, now, as to that, may I offer a suggestion? Bearing in mind that Ermentrude is still not completely recovered, and the discomforts you are living in, would you consider...?'

Emmy and her mother, left on their own, rummaged around, finding blankets and pillows. 'There's a mattress in the little bedroom upstairs, if you could manage on that for a few nights,' suggested Mrs Foster worriedly. 'If only they would take all this furniture away...'

Emmy, making up some sort of a bed, declared that she would be quite all right. 'It won't be for long,' she said cheerfully. 'I'll be more comfortable here than I was in London. And Father's got his job—that's what matters.'

She went downstairs to feed the animals. 'The professor and Charlie are a long time,' she observed. 'I hope Charlie hasn't got lost. It's almost tea time, too, and I'm sure he wants to get back to London.'

The professor wasn't lost, nor was Charlie. Having concluded his talk with Mr Foster, the professor had whistled to his dog and set off for a walk, having agreed to return to the school when Mr Foster should be free to return home.

The unpleasant weather hadn't improved at all. Sleet and wet snow fell from time to time from a grey sky rapidly darkening, and the lanes he walked along were half-frozen mud. He was unaware of the weather, his thoughts miles away.

'I am, of course, mad,' he told Charlie. 'No man in his right senses would have conceived such a plan without due regard to the pitfalls and disadvantages. And what is Anneliese going to think?'

Upon reflection he thought that he didn't much mind what she felt. She had been sufficiently well brought up to treat his guests civilly, and if she and Ermentrude were to cross swords he felt reasonably sure that Ermentrude would give as good as she got. Besides, Anneliese wouldn't be staying at his home, although he expected to see a good deal of her.

He waited patiently while Charlie investigated a tree. Surely Anneliese would understand that he couldn't leave Ermentrude and her parents to spend Christmas in a house brim-full of someone else's furniture and inadequate plumbing, especially as he had been the means of their move there in the first place. Perhaps he had rather over-emphasised Ermentrude's need to recuperate after concussion, but it had successfully decided her father to accept his offer.

He strode back to the school to meet Mr Foster and accompany him back to the lodge.

Emmy was making tea when they got there.

'You're wet,' she said unnecessarily. 'And you'll be very late back home. I've made toast, and there's a bowl of food for Charlie when you've dried him off. There's an old towel hanging on the back of the kitchen door. Give me that coat; I'll hang it on a chair by the Aga or you'll catch your death of cold.'

The professor, meekly doing as he was told, reflected that Ermentrude sounded just like a wife. He tried to imagine Anneliese talking like that and failed, but then she would never allow herself to be in a situation such as Emmy was now. She would have demanded to be taken to the nearest hotel. He laughed at the thought, and Emmy looked round at him in surprise. The professor didn't laugh often.

He helped her father out of his wet jacket, poured the tea and called her mother, who was hanging curtains in the small bedroom.

'They'll have to do,' she said, coming into the kitchen. 'I've pinned them up for the moment, and it does make the room look cosier.'

She smiled at the professor. 'Did you have a nice walk? Do sit down. Let Charlie lie by the stove; he must be tired. It's a wretched evening for you to travel.'

Emmy handed round toast and a pot of jam. The tea, in an assortment of cups and saucers, was hot and strong. She watched the professor spread jam on his toast and take a bite, and thought of Beaker's dainty teas with the fine china and little cakes. He looked up and caught her eye and smiled.

Mr Foster drank his tea and put down his cup. 'Professor ter Mennolt has made us a most generous offer. He considers that Emmy needs rest after her accident, and that as a medical man he cannot like the idea of her remaining here while the house is in such a state of confusion. He has most kindly offered to take us over to Holland for the Christmas period to stay in his house there. He will be going the day after tomorrow—'

'You said tomorrow…' interrupted Emmy.

'I find that I am unable to get away until the following day,' said the professor smoothly. 'But I shall be delighted to have you as my guests for a few days. Hopefully by the time you return the problems in this house will be resolved.' He added blandly, 'As a doctor, I would feel it very wrong of me to allow Ermentrude to stay here until she is quite fit.'

Emmy drew a deep breath. She didn't think he meant a word of it; he might look and sound like the learned man he undoubtedly was but his suggestion was preposterous. Besides, there was nothing wrong with her. She opened her mouth to say so and closed it again, swallowing her protest. She didn't stand a chance against that weighty professional manner.

She listened to her mother receiving his offer with delighted relief.

'Surely we shall upset your plans for Christmas? Your family and guests? How will you let them know? And all the extra work…'

The professor sounded reassuring. 'I'm sure you don't need to worry, Mrs Foster. If you can face the idea of Christmas in Holland, I can assure you that you will all be most welcome. Rather short notice, I'm afraid, but if you could manage to be ready by midday on the day after tomorrow?'

Mr and Mrs Foster exchanged glances. It was an offer they could hardly refuse. On their way they would have scrambled through the festive season somehow or other, always hopeful that Mr Bennett's furniture would have been moved by the time Emmy arrived. But now that seemed unlikely, and with Christmas in such a muddle, and Emmy not quite herself...

Mrs Foster said simply, 'Thank you for a most generous offer; we accept with pleasure. Only don't let us interfere with any of your family arrangements. I mean, we are happy just to have a bed and a roof over our heads...'

The professor smiled. 'It will be a pleasure to have you—I always think the more the merrier at Christmas, don't you?'

'Your family will be there?'

'I have two sisters with children and a younger brother. I'm sure they will be delighted to meet you.'

He got up. 'You will forgive me if I leave you now?'

He shook hands with Mr and Mrs Foster, but Ermentrude he patted on the shoulder in a casual manner and told her to take care.

When he had gone, Mrs Foster said, 'What a delightful man, and how kind he is. You know, Emmy, your father and I were at our wits' end wondering what to do about Christmas, and along comes Professor ter Mennolt and settles it all for us—just like that.'

Mr Foster was watching Emmy's face. 'A good man, and very well thought of in his profession, I believe. He tells me that he is engaged to be married. I dare say we shall meet his fiancée.'

Emmy said in a bright voice, 'Oh, I have met her—she came to St Luke's one day to see him—she'd been staying over here. She's beautiful, you know. Fair and slender, and has the most gorgeous clothes.'

'Did you like her?' asked her mother.

'No,' said Emmy. 'But I expect that was because she was the kind of person I would like to be and aren't.'

'Well,' said her mother briskly, 'let's get tidied up here and then think about what clothes to take with us. I've that long black skirt and that rather nice crêpe de Chine blouse; that'll do for the evening. What about you, Emmy?'

'Well, there's the brown velvet; that'll do.' It would have to; she had no other suitable dress for the evening. She thought for a moment. 'I could go in the jacket and skirt, and wear my coat over them. A blouse or two, and a sweater...I don't suppose we'll be there for more than a few days.'

'If we sell the house, you shall have some new clothes, and now your father's got this splendid post...'

'Oh, I've plenty of clothes,' said Emmy airily. 'And they don't matter. It's marvellous that Father's here, and this is a dear little house.'

She looked round her at the muddle—chairs stacked in corners, a wardrobe in the hall, Mr Bennett's piano still in the sitting room. They looked at each other and burst out laughing. 'When you're able to settle in,' said Emmy.

The professor, with Charlie beside him, drove back to Chelsea. 'I do not know what possessed me,' he told his companion. 'Anneliese is not going to like my unexpected guests, and yet what else could I do? Would you like to spend Christmas in such cold chaos? No, of course you wouldn't. Common humanity dictated that I should do something about it... Let me think...'

By the time he had reached his home his plans were made. Over the dinner which Beaker set before him he went through them carefully, and presently went to his study and picked up the phone.

Beaker, bringing his coffee later, coughed gently. 'Mrs Burge and I, sir, we miss Miss Foster.'

The professor looked at him over his spectacles. 'So do I, Beaker. By the way, she and her parents are going to Holland with me for Christmas. Due to unavoidable circumstances, the house they have moved to is unfit to live in for the moment and they have nowhere to go.'

Beaker's face remained impassive. 'A good idea, if I may say so, sir. The young lady isn't quite herself after that nasty attack.'

'Just so, Beaker. I shan't be leaving until the day after tomorrow—pack a few things for me, will you? Enough for a week.'

Beaker gone, the professor buried his commanding nose in a weighty tome and forgot everything else. It was only as he was going to bed that he remembered that he should have phoned Anneliese. It would be better to tell her when he got to Holland, perhaps. He felt sure that she would be as warmly welcoming to his unexpected guests as his sisters had promised to be.

Emmy slept badly; a mattress on the floor, surrounded by odds and ends of furniture which creaked and sighed during the night, was hardly conducive to a restful night. Nor were her thoughts—largely of the professor—none of which were of a sensible nature.

She got up heavy-eyed and her mother said, 'The professor is quite right, Emmy, you don't look at all yourself.' She eyed her much loved daughter worriedly. 'Was it very uncomfortable on the mattress? There's no room to put up a bed, and anyway we haven't got one until we can get yours from the house in London. Your father can sleep there tonight and you can come in with me…'

'I was very comfortable,' said Emmy. 'But there was such a lot to think about that I didn't sleep very well. I expect I'm excited.'

Mrs Foster put the eggs for breakfast on to boil. 'So am I. We'll pack presently—your father's going up to the school to find out where the nearest kennels are, then he can take these three later this evening.'

'I hope they'll be all right, but it's only for a few days. Wouldn't it be marvellous if we came back and found all Mr Bennett's furniture gone and the plumbing repaired?'

'We mustn't expect too much, but it would be nice. Directly after Christmas your father will go up to London and see the estate agent and arrange for your bed to be brought down here. You need never go back there unless you want to, Emmy.' Her mother turned round to smile at her. 'Oh, Emmy, isn't it all too good to be true?'

There was a good deal to do—cases to pack, hair to wash, hands to be attended to.

'I do hope the professor won't feel ashamed of us,' said Mrs Foster.

Emmy said quite passionately, 'No, Mother, he's not like that. He's kind and, and—' She paused. 'Well, he's nice.' And, when her mother gave her a surprised look, she added, 'He's quite tiresome at times too.'

Mrs Foster wisely said nothing.

They all went to bed early in a house strangely silent now that George and Snoodles and Enoch had been taken, protesting fiercely, to the kennels near Shaftesbury. Emmy had another wakeful night, worrying about her clothes and whether the professor might be regretting his generosity— and what would Anneliese think when she knew? She dropped off finally and had a nightmare, wherein his family, grotesquely hideous, shouted abuse at her. She was only too glad when it was time to get up.

They made the house as secure as they could, piling the furniture tidily under the tarpaulins and tying them down, parking her father's car as near the house as possible and covering it with more tarpaulins. There was just time to have a cup of coffee before the professor was due to arrive.

He came punctually, relaxed and pleasant, drank the coffee he was offered, stowed the luggage in the boot and invited everyone to get into the car.

Mr Foster was told to sit in front, for, as the professor pointed out, he might need directions. 'We're going from Dover—the hovercraft. It's quick, and there is quite a long journey on the other side.'

He got in and turned to look at Mrs Foster. 'Passports?' he asked. 'Keys and so forth? So easily forgotten at the last minute, and I have rushed you.'

'I think we've got everything, Professor…'

'Would you call me Ruerd?' His glance slid over Emmy's rather pale face, but he didn't say anything to her.

It was another cold day but it wasn't raining, although the sky was dark. The professor drove steadily, going across country to pick up the motorway outside Southampton and turning inland at Chichester to pick up the A27 and then the A259. He stopped in Hawkshurst at a pub in the little town where they had soup and sandwiches.

'Are we in good time for the hovercraft,' asked Mrs Foster anxiously.

'Plenty of time,' he assured her. 'It takes longer this way, I believe, but the motorway up to London and down to Dover would have been packed with traffic.'

'You've been this way before?' asked Emmy's father.

'No, but it seemed a good route. On a fine day it must

be very pleasant. I dislike motorways, but I have to use them frequently.'

They drove on presently, joining the A20 as they neared Dover. From the warmth of the car Emmy surveyed the wintry scene outside. How awful if she was to be seasick…

She forgot about it in the excitement of going on board, and, once there, since it was rather like sitting in a superior bus, she forgot about feeling sick and settled down beside her mother, sharing the tea they had been brought and eating the biscuits. Her father had gone to sleep and the professor, with a word of apology, had taken out some papers from a pocket, put on his spectacles and was absorbing their contents.

It was rough but not unbearably so. All the same it was nice to get back into the car.

'Not too tired?' asked the professor, and, once clear of the traffic around Calais, sent the car surging forward, out of France and into Belgium, where he took the road to Ghent and then on into Holland.

Emmy looked out of the window and thought the country looked rather flat and uninteresting. Instead she studied the back of the professor's head, and wished that she were sitting beside him. She caught the thought up short before it could go any further. All this excitement was going to her head, and any silly ideas must be squashed at once. Circumstances had thrown them together; circumstances would very shortly part them. That was an end of that.

She sighed, and then choked on a breath when the professor asked, 'What's the matter, Ermentrude?'

She had forgotten that he could see her in his mirror above the dashboard. 'Nothing, nothing,' she repeated. 'I'm fine. It's all very interesting.'

Which, considering it was now almost dark and the view held no interest whatsoever, was a silly answer.

It was completely dark by the time he turned in at his own gates and she saw the lights streaming from the house ahead of them. She hadn't expected anything like this. A substantial villa, perhaps, or a roomy townhouse, but not this large, square house, with its big windows and imposing front door.

As they got out of the car the door opened and Solly and Tip dashed out, barking a welcome—a welcome offered in a more sedate fashion by Cokker, who greeted the guests as though three people arriving for Christmas without more than a few hours' warning was an everyday occurrence.

The hall was warm and splendidly lighted and there was a Christmas tree in one corner, not yet decorated. Cokker took coats and scarves, and the whole party crossed the hall and went into the drawing room.

'Oh, what a beautiful room!' said Mrs Foster.

'I'm glad you like it. Shall we have a drink before you go to your rooms? Would dinner in half an hour suit you?'

'Yes, please.' Mrs Foster beamed at him. 'I don't know about anyone else, but I'm famished.' She sat down by the fire and looked around her, frankly admiring. 'Ruerd, this is so beautiful and yet you choose to live a good part of your life in England?'

'I go where my work is,' he told her, smiling. 'I'm very happy in Chelsea, but this is my home.'

He crossed to the drinks table and went to sit by Mr Foster, talking about their journey, leaving Emmy to sit with her mother. Presently Cokker came, and with him a tall, stout woman, no longer young but very upright.

'Ah, Tiele,' said the professor. 'My housekeeper and Cokker's wife. She doesn't speak English but I'm sure you will manage very well.'

He said something to her in what Emmy supposed was Dutch.

'Tiele is from Friesland, so we speak Friese together…'

'You're not Dutch? You're Frisian?' asked Emmy.

'I had a Friesian grandmother,' he told her. 'Tiele will take you upstairs, and when you are ready will you come back here again? Don't hurry; you must be tired.'

On their way to the door Emmy stopped by him. 'Aren't you tired?' she asked him.

He smiled down at her. 'No. When I'm with people I like or doing something I enjoy I'm never tired.'

He smiled slowly and she turned away and followed her mother, father and Tiele up the wide, curving staircase. It was inevitable, I suppose, she thought, that sooner or later I should fall in love with him. Only it's a pity I couldn't have waited until we were back home and there would be no chance of seeing him again. I must, decided Emmy firmly, be very circumspect in my manner towards him.

There were a number of rooms leading from the gallery which encircled the stairs. Emmy watched her parents disappear into one at the front of the house before she was led by Tiele to a room on the opposite side. It was not a very large room, but it was furnished beautifully with a canopied bed, a William the Fourth dressing table in tulip wood, two Georgian *bergères* upholstered in the same pale pink of the curtains and bedspread, and a mahogany bedside table—an elegant Georgian trifle.

The one long window opened onto a small wrought-iron balcony; she peeped out onto the dark outside and turned back thankfully to the cheerful light of the rose-shaded lamps. There was a clothes cupboard too, built into one wall, and a small, quite perfect bathroom.

Emmy prowled around, picking things up and putting them down again. 'I wonder,' she said out loud, 'if Anneliese knows how lucky she is?'

She tidied herself then, brushed her hair, powdered her nose and went to fetch her parents.

'Darling,' said her mother worriedly. 'Should we have come? I mean, just look at everything…'

Her father said sensibly, 'This is Ruerd's home, my dear, and he has made us welcome. Never mind if it is a mansion or a cottage. I fancy that it is immaterial to him, and it should be to us.'

They went down to the drawing room and found the professor standing before his hearth, the dogs pressed up against him.

'You have all you want?' he asked Mrs Foster. 'Do say if you need anything, won't you? I rushed you here with very little time to decide what to pack.

When Cokker came the professor said, 'I believe dinner is on the table. And if you aren't too tired later, sir, I'd like to show you some first editions I have. I recently found Robert Herrick's *Hesperides*—seventeenth century, but perhaps you would advise me as to the exact date?'

The dining room was as magnificent as the drawing room, with a pedestal table in mahogany ringed around by twelve chairs, those at the head and foot of the table being carvers upholstered in red leather. It was a large room, with plenty of space for the massive side table along one wall and the small serving table facing it.

There were a number of paintings on the walls. Emmy, anxious not to appear nosy, determined to have a good look at them when there was no one about. At the moment she was delighted to keep her attention on the delicious food she was being offered. Smoked salmon with wafer-thin brown bread and butter, roast pheasant with game chips and an assortment of vegetables, and following these a *crème brûlée*.

They had coffee in the drawing room and presently the professor took Mr Foster away to his library, first of all wishing Mrs Foster and Emmy a good night. 'Breakfast is at half past eight, but if you would like to have it in bed you have only to say so. Sleep well.' His gaze dwelt on Emmy's face for a moment and she looked away quickly.

She was going to stay awake, she thought, lying in a scented bath. There were a great many problems to mull over—and the most important one was how to forget the professor as quickly as possible. If it's only infatuation, she thought, I can get over it once I've stopped seeing him.

She got into bed and lay admiring her surroundings before putting out the bedside light, prepared to lie awake and worry. She had reckoned without the comfort of the bed and the long day behind her. With a last dreamy thought of the professor, she slept.

CHAPTER SEVEN

EMMY was wakened in the morning by a sturdy young girl in a coloured pinafore, bearing a tray of tea. She beamed at Emmy, drew the curtains back, giggled cheerfully and went away.

Emmy drank her tea and hopped out of bed intent on looking out of the window. She opened it and stepped cautiously onto the balcony. The tiles were icy and her toes curled under with the cold, but the air was fresh and smelled of the sea.

She took great gulping breaths and peered down to the garden below. It was more than a garden; it stretched away towards what looked like rough grass, and beyond that she could glimpse the sea. She took her fill of the view and then looked down again. Directly under the balcony the professor was standing, looking up at her, the dogs beside him.

He wished her good morning. 'And go and put some clothes on, Ermentrude, and come outside.' He laughed then.

She said haughtily, 'Good morning, Professor. I think not, thank you. I'm cold.'

'Well, of course you are with only a nightie on. Get dressed and come on down. You need the exercise.'

Emmy felt light-headed at the sight of him, standing there, laughing at her.

She said, 'All right, ten minutes,' and whisked herself back into her room, leaving the professor wondering why the sight of her in a sensible nightdress with her hair hanging untidily in a cloud around her shoulders, should so disturb him in a way which Anneliese, even in the most exquisite gown, never had. He reminded himself that Anneliese would be coming to dinner that evening, and regretted the impulse to invite Emmy to join him.

She came through the side door to meet him, wrapped in her coat, a scarf over her hair, sensible shoes on her feet. Tip and Solly made much of her, and she said, 'Oh, what a pity that Charlie isn't here, too.'

'I think that Beaker might not like that. Charlie is his darling, as much loved as Humphrey.'

They had begun to walk down the length of the garden, and at its end he opened a wicket gate and led the way over rough grass until they reached the edge of the dunes with the sea beyond. There was a strong wind blowing, whipping the waves high, turning the water to a tumultuous steel-grey.

The professor put an arm round Emmy's shoulders to steady her. 'Like it?'

'Oh, yes, it's heavenly! And so quiet—I mean, no people, no cars...'

'Just us,' said the professor.

It wasn't full daylight, but she could see the wide sand stretching away on either side of them, disappearing into the early-morning gloom.

'You could walk for miles,' said Emmy. 'How far?'

'All the way to den Helder in the north and to the Hoek in the south.'

'You must think of this when you are in London…'

'Yes. I suppose that one day I'll come to live here permanently.'

'I expect you will want to do that when you're married and have a family,' said Emmy, and felt the pain which the words were giving her. Would Anneliese stand here with him, watching the stormy sea and blown by the wind? And his children? She pictured a whole clutch of them and dismissed the thought. Anneliese would have one child—two, perhaps—but no more than that.

She felt tears well under her eyelids. Ruerd would be a splendid father and his home was large enough to accommodate a whole bunch of children, but that would never happen.

'You're crying,' said the professor. 'Why?'

'It's the wind; it makes my eyes water. The air is like sucking ice cubes from the fridge, isn't it?'

He smiled then. 'An apt description. Let us go back and have breakfast before we decorate the tree—a morning's work. We will come again—whatever the weather, it is always a splendid view.

Breakfast was a cheerful meal; her parents had slept well and the talk was wholly of Christmas and the forthcoming gaiety.

'My sisters will come later today, my brother tomorrow. Anneliese—my fiancée—will be coming this evening to dinner.'

'We look forward to meeting her,' said Mrs Foster, politely untruthful. Maternal instinct warned her that Anneliese wasn't going to like finding them at Ruerd's house. Although from all accounts she had nothing to fear from Emmy, thought Mrs Foster sadly. A darling girl, but with no looks. A man as handsome as Ruerd would surely choose a beautiful woman for his wife.

They decorated the tree after breakfast, hanging it with glass baubles, tinsel, little china angels and a great many fairy lights. On top, of course, there was a fairy doll—given after Christmas to the youngest of his nieces, the professor told them.

'You have several nieces?' asked Mrs Foster.

'Three so far, and four nephews. I do hope you like children…'

'Indeed I do. Ruerd, we feel terrible at not having any presents to give.'

'Please don't worry about that. They have so many gifts that they lose count as to whom they are from.'

Emmy, making paper chains for the nursery, found him beside her.

'After lunch we'll go over the house, if you would like that, but, in the meantime, will you bring those upstairs and we'll hang them before the children get here?'

The nursery was at the back of the house behind a baize door. There was a night nursery, too, and a bedroom for nanny, a small kitchenette and a splendidly equipped bathroom.

'The children sleep here, but they go where they like in the house. Children should be with their parents as much as possible, don't you agree?'

'Well, of course. Otherwise they're not a family, are they?' She stood there, handing him the chains as he fastened them in festoons between the walls. 'Did you sleep here, too?'

'Oh, yes. Until I was eight years old. On our eighth birthdays we were given our own bedrooms.'

He hung the chains, and turned to stare at her. 'You like my home, Ermentrude?'

'Yes, indeed I do. I think you must be very happy here.'

She walked to the door, uneasy under his look. 'At what time do your sisters arrive?'

His voice was reassuringly casual again. 'Very shortly after lunch. It will be chaos for the rest of the afternoon, I expect. Several friends will be coming to dinner.'

She paused as they reached the stairs. 'You have been so kind to us, Professor, but that doesn't mean you have to include us in your family gatherings.' She saw his quick frown. 'I've put that badly, but you know quite well what I mean, don't you? Mother and Father and I would be quite happy if you would like us to dine alone. I mean, you weren't expecting us...'

She had made him angry. She started down the staircase and wished that she had held her tongue, but she had had to say it. Perhaps if she hadn't fallen in love with him she wouldn't have felt the urge to make it clear to him that they were on sufferance, even if it was a kindly sufferance.

He put out a hand and stopped her, turned her round to face him, and when he spoke it was in a rigidly controlled voice which masked his anger.

'Never say such a thing to me again, Ermentrude. You and your parents are my guests, and welcome in my house. Be good enough to remember that.'

She stood quietly under his hand. 'All right, I won't,' she told him. 'Don't be so annoyed, there's no need.'

He smiled then. 'Should I beg your pardon? Did I startle you?'

'Oh, no. I think I've always known that you conceal your feelings.' She met his look and went pink. 'Now it's me who should say sorry. Goodness me, I wouldn't have dared talk to you like that at St Luke's. It must be because we're here.'

He studied her face, nodded and went on down the stairs, his hand still on her arm.

* * *

Lunch was a cheerful meal. The professor and Mr Foster seemed to have a great deal in common; neither was at a loss for a subject although they were careful to include Mrs Foster and Emmy.

Shortly afterwards the first of the guests arrived. The house seemed suddenly to be full of children, racing around, shouting and laughing, hugging the dogs, hanging onto their uncle, absorbing Emmy and her parents into their lives as though they had always been there.

There were only four of them but it seemed more— three boys and a girl, the eldest six years and the youngest two. A rather fierce Scottish nanny came with them, but she took one look at Emmy's unassuming person and allowed her to be taken over by her charges. So Emmy was coaxed to go to the nursery with the children and their mother, a tall young woman with the professor's good looks. She had shaken Emmy by the hand, and liked her.

'Joke,' she said with a smile. 'It sounds like part of an egg but it's spelt like a joke. I do hope you like children. Mine run wild at Christmas, and Ruerd spoils them. My sister Alemke will be here shortly; she's got a boy and two girls, and a baby on the way.' She grinned at Emmy. 'Are we all a bit overpowering?'

'No, no. I like children. Only, you see, the professor is so—well, remote at the hospital. It's hard to think of him with a family.'

'I know just what you mean.' Joke made a face. 'He loves children, but I don't think Anneliese, his fiancée, likes them very much. I sound critical, don't I? Well, I am. Why he has to marry someone like her I'll never know. Suitable, I suppose.'

She took Emmy's arm. 'I'm so glad you're here. Only I hope the children aren't going to plague you.'

'I shan't mind a bit. How old are your sister's children?'

'The boy is five, and the girls—twins—almost three. Let's go down and have tea.'

Her sister had arrived when they got down to the drawing room and there were more children, who, undeterred by language problems, took possession of Emmy.

Alemke was very like her sister, only younger. 'Isn't this fun?' she said in English as good as Emmy's own. 'I love a crowd. Our husbands will come later, and I suppose Aunt Beatrix will be here and Uncle Cor and Grandmother ter Mennolt. She's a bit fierce, but don't mind her. There'll be Ruerd's friends, too; it should be great fun. And Anneliese, of course.'

The sisters exchanged looks. 'We don't like her, though we try very hard to do so,' said Joke.

'She's very beautiful,' said Emmy, anxious to be fair.

'You've met her?'

'She came to St Luke's when I was working there, to see the professor.'

'Do you always call Ruerd "professor"?' asked Joke.

'Well, yes. He's—he's… Well, it's difficult to explain, but the hospital— He's a senior consultant and I was on the telephone exchange.'

Alemke took her arm. 'Come over here and sit with us while we have tea, and tell us about the hospital—wasn't there a bomb or something? Ruerd mentioned it vaguely. Anneliese was over there, wasn't she?'

Emmy accepted a delicate china cup of tea and a tiny biscuit.

'Yes, it must have been very difficult for the professor because, of course, he was busier than usual.'

Joke and Alemke exchanged a quick look. Here was the answer to their prayers. This small girl with the plain face and the beautiful eyes was exactly what they had in mind for their brother. They had seen with satisfaction that, beyond a few civil remarks, he had avoided Emmy and she had gone out of her way to stay at the other end of the room. A good sign, but it was unfortunate that Ruerd had given his promise to Anneliese. Who would be coming that evening, no doubt looking more beautiful than ever.

The children, excited but sleepy, were led away after tea to be bathed and given supper and be put to bed, and everyone else went away to dress for the evening. Emmy had seen with pleasure that her parents were enjoying themselves and were perfectly at ease in their grand surroundings. She reminded herself that before her father had been made redundant he and her mother had had a pleasant social life. It was only when they had gone to London and he had been out of work that they had had to change their ways.

Emmy took a long time dressing. The result looked very much as usual to her anxious eyes as she studied her person in the pier-glass. The brown dress was best described as useful, its colour mouse-like, guaranteed to turn the wearer into a nonentity, its modest style such that it could be worn year after year without even being noticed.

Emmy had bought it at a sale, searching for a dress to wear to the annual hospital ball at St Luke's two years previously, knowing that it would have to last for a number of years even if its outings were scanty. It hardly added to her looks, although it couldn't disguise her pretty figure.

She went slowly down the staircase, hoping that no one would notice her.

The professor noticed—and knew then why Emmy hadn't wanted to join his other guests. He crossed the hall to meet her at the foot of the staircase, and took her hand with a smile and a nod at her person. He said in exactly the right tone of casual approval, 'Very nice, Ermentrude. Come and meet the rest of my guests.'

His brothers-in-law were there now, but he took her first to an old lady sitting by the console table.

'Aunt Beatrix, this is Ermentrude Foster who is staying here over Christmas with her parents—you have already met them.'

The old lady looked her up and down and held out a hand. 'Ah, yes. You have an unusual name. Perhaps you are an unusual girl?'

Emmy shook the old hand. 'No, no. I'm very ordinary.'

Aunt Beatrix patted the stool at her feet. 'Sit down and tell me what you do.' She shot a glance at Emmy. 'You do do something?'

'Well, yes.' Emmy told her of the job at St. Luke's. 'But, now Father has a post in Dorset, I can live there and find something to do while I train.'

'What for?'

'I want to embroider—really complicated embroidery, you know? Tapestry work and smocking on babies' dresses and drawn thread work. And when I know enough I'd like to open a small shop.'

'Not get married?'

'I expect if someone asked me, and I loved him, I'd like to get married,' said Emmy.

The professor had wandered back. 'Come and meet Rik and Hugo and the others.' He put a hand on her shoulder and led her from one to the other, and then paused by Anneliese, who was superb in red chiffon, delicately made-up, her hair an artless mass of loose curls.

'Remember Ermentrude?' asked the professor cheerfully.

'Of course I do.' Anneliese studied the brown dress slowly and smiled a nasty little smile. 'What a rush for you, coming here at a moment's notice. Ruerd told me all about it, of course. You must feel very grateful to him. Such a bore for you, having no time to buy some decent clothes. Still, I suppose you're only here for a couple of days.'

'Yes, I expect we are,' said Emmy in a carefully controlled voice. Just then the professor was called away. Anneliese turned round and spoke to a tall, stout woman chatting nearby. 'Mother, come and meet this girl Ruerd is helping yet again.'

Mevrouw van Moule ignored the hand Emmy put out. She had cold eyes and a mean mouth, and Emmy thought, In twenty years' time Anneliese will look like that.

'I dare say you find all this rather awkward, do you not? You worked in a hospital, I understand.'

'Yes,' said Emmy pleasantly. 'An honest day's work, like the professor. He does an honest day's work, too.' She smiled sweetly at Anneliese. 'What kind of work do you do, Anneliese?'

'Anneliese is far too delicate and sensitive to work,' declared her mother. 'In any case she has no need to do so. She will marry Professor ter Mennolt very shortly.'

'Yes, I did know.' Emmy smiled at them both. It was a difficult thing to do; she wanted to slap them, and shake Anneliese until her teeth rattled in her head. 'So nice to see you again,' she told Anneliese, and crossed the room to join her mother and father, who were talking to an elderly couple, cousins of the professor.

The professor's two sisters, watching her from the other end of the room, saw her pink cheeks and lifted chin and wondered what Anneliese had said to her. When the professor joined them for a moment, Joke said, 'Ruerd, why did you leave Emmy with Anneliese and her mother? They've upset her. You know how nasty Anneliese can be.'

She caught her brother's eye. 'All right, I shouldn't have said that. But her mother's there, too…'

She wandered away and presently fetched up beside Emmy.

'You crossed swords,' she said into Emmy's ear. 'Were they absolutely awful?'

'Yes.'

'I hope you gave them as good as you got,' said Joke.

'Well, no. I wanted to very badly, but I couldn't, could I? I'm a guest here, aren't I? And I couldn't answer back.'

'Why not?'

'Anneliese is going to marry Ruerd. He—he must love her, and it would hurt him if she were upset.'

Joke tucked her hand in her arm. 'Emmy, dear, would you mind if Ruerd was upset?'

'Yes, of course. He's—he's kind and patient and very generous, and he deserves to be happy.' Emmy looked at Joke, unaware of the feelings showing so plainly in her face.

'Yes, he does,' said Joke gravely. 'Come and meet some more of the family. We're endless, aren't we? Have you met my grandmother?'

Twenty people sat down to dinner presently. The table had been extended and more chairs arranged round it, but there was still plenty of room. Emmy, sitting between one of the brothers-in-law and a jovial man—an old friend of the family—could see her parents on the other side of the table, obviously enjoying themselves.

The professor sat at the head of the table, of course, with Anneliese beside him and his grandmother on his other hand. Emmy looked away and concentrated on something else. There was plenty to concentrate upon. The table for a start, with the lace table mats, sparkling glass and polished silver. There was an epergne at its centre, filled with holly, Christmas roses and trailing ivy, and candles in silver candelabra.

Dinner lived up to the splendour of the table: sorrel soup, mustard-grilled sole, raised game pie with braised celery, brussel sprouts with chestnuts, spinach purée and creamed potatoes, and to follow a selection of desserts.

Emmy, finding it difficult to choose between a mouth-watering trifle and a milanaise soufflé, remembered the bread and jam they had once eaten and blushed. She blushed again when the professor caught her eye and smiled. Perhaps he had remembered, too, although how he had thought of anything else but his beautiful Anneliese sitting beside him…

Emmy, savouring the trifle, saw that Anneliese was toying with a water ice. No wonder she was so slim. Not slim, thought Emmy—bony. And, however gorgeous her dress was, it didn't disguise Anneliese's lack of bosom. Listening politely to the old friend of the family talking about his garden, Emmy was thankfully aware that her own bosom left nothing to be desired. A pity about the brown dress, of course, but, since the professor had barely glanced at her, it hardly mattered—a potato sack would have done just as well.

Dinner over, the party repaired to the drawing room and Emmy went to sit by her mother.

Mrs Foster was enjoying herself. 'This is delightful, Emmy. When I think that we might still be at the lodge, surrounded by someone else's furniture… I do wish we had brought a present for Ruerd.'

'Well, there wasn't time, Mother. Perhaps we can send him something when we get back home. Has he said how long we're staying here?'

'No, but he told your father that he has to return to England on Boxing Day, so I expect we shall go back with him then.' Mrs Foster added, 'I don't like his fiancée; she'll not make him a good wife.'

They were joined by other guests then, and the rest of the evening passed pleasantly enough. Around midnight Anneliese and her mother went home. She went from one group to the other, laughing and talking, her hand on the professor's sleeve, barely pausing to wish Emmy and her mother goodnight.

'I'll be back tomorrow,' she told them. 'Ruerd has excellent servants but they need supervision. So fortunate that Ruerd offered you a roof over your heads for Christmas. Of course, it was the least anyone could do.'

She gave them a brittle smile and left them.

'I don't like her,' said Mrs Foster softly.

'She's beautiful,' said Emmy. 'She will be a most suitable wife for Ruerd.'

Alemke joined them then and they chattered together, presently joined by several other guests, until people began to drift home. All this while the professor had contrived to be at the other end of the room, going from one group to the other, pausing briefly to say something to Mrs Foster, hoping that Emmy was enjoying herself. The perfect host.

The next day was Christmas Eve, and Anneliese arrived for lunch wrapped in cashmere and a quilted silk jacket. At least she came alone this time, playing her part as the future mistress of Ruerd's house with a charm which set Emmy's teeth on edge.

Somehow she managed to make Emmy feel that she was receiving charity, even while she smiled and talked and ordered Cokker about as though she were already his mistress. He was called away to the phone, and she took the opportunity to alter the arrangements for lunch, re-

primand Cokker for some trivial fault and point out to
Emmy in a sugary voice that there would be guests for
lunch and had she nothing more suitable to wear?

'No, I haven't,' said Emmy coldly. 'And if you don't
wish to sit down to the table with me, please say so. I'm
sure the professor won't mind if I and my mother and
father have something on a tray in another room.' She
added, 'I'll go and find him and tell him so…'

Anneliese said urgently, 'No, no, I didn't mean… It
was only a suggestion. I'm sure you look quite nice, and
everyone knows—'

'What does everyone know?' asked the professor
from the door.

He looked from one to the other of them, and Emmy
said in a wooden voice, 'Oh, you must ask Anneliese that,'
and went past him out of the room.

The professor said quietly, 'The Fosters are my guests,
Anneliese. I hope that you remember that—and that you
are in my house!'

She leaned up to kiss his cheek. 'Dear Ruerd, of course
I remember. But Emmy isn't happy, you know; this isn't
her kind of life. She told me just now that she and her
parents would be much happier having lunch by themselves. I told her that she looked quite nice—she's so sensitive about her clothes—and that everyone knew they had
no time to pack sufficient clothes.'

She shrugged her shoulders. 'I've done my best, Ruerd.'
She flashed him a smile. 'I'm going to talk to your sisters;
I've hardly had time to speak to them.'

The professor stood for a moment after she had left
him, deep in thought. Then he wandered off, away from
the drawing room where everyone was having a drink
before lunch, opening and closing doors quietly until he

found Emmy in the garden room, standing by the great stone sink, doing nothing.

He closed the door behind him and stood leaning against it. 'You know, Emmy, it doesn't really matter in the least what clothes you are wearing. Anneliese tells me that you feel inadequately dressed and are shy of joining my guests. I do know that clothes matter to a woman, but the woman wearing them matters much more.

'Everyone likes you, Emmy, and you know me well enough by now to know that I don't say anything I don't mean. Indeed, they like you so much that Joke wants you to stay a few weeks and help her with the children while Nanny goes on holiday. Would you consider that? I shall be in England, Rik has to go to Switzerland for ten days on business, and she would love to have your company and help.'

Emmy had had her back to him, but she turned round now. 'I wouldn't believe a word of that if it was someone else, but you wouldn't lie to me, would you?'

'No, Emmy.'

'Joke would really like me to stay and help with the children? I'd like that very much. But what about Mother and Father?'

'I'll take them back when I go in two days' time. Probably by then the problem of the furniture will have been settled.' He smiled. 'They will have everything as they want it by the time you get back.'

'I'll stay if Joke would like that,' said Emmy.

'She'll be delighted. Now come and eat your lunch— we will talk to your mother and father presently.'

She sat next to him at lunch, with Rik on her other side and Hugo across the table, and between them they had her laughing and talking, all thoughts of her clothes forgotten.

That afternoon she went for a walk with Joke and Alemke and the children, down to the village and back again, walking fast in a cold wind and under a grey sky.

'There'll be snow later,' said Joke. 'Will you come to church tomorrow, Emmy? The family goes, and anyone else who'd like to. We have midday lunch and a gigantic feast in the evening. The children stay up for it and it's bedlam.'

There was tea round the fire when they got back, with Anneliese acting as hostess, although, when Joke and Alemke joined the others, she said with a titter, 'Oh, dear, I shouldn't be doing this—Joke, do forgive me. I am so used to being here that sometimes I feel that I am already married.'

Several people gave her a surprised look, but no one said anything until Alemke started to talk about their walk.

The professor wasn't there and neither, Emmy saw, were her mother and father. She wondered if Anneliese knew that she had been asked to stay on after Christmas and decided that she didn't—for Anneliese was being gracious, talking to her in her rather loud voice, saying how glad she would be to be back in her own house, and did she know what kind of job she hoped to get?

Emmy ate Christmas cake and said placidly that she had no idea. Her heart ached with love for Ruerd but nothing of that showed in her serene face, nicely flushed by her walk.

She didn't have to suffer Anneliese's condescending conversation for long; she was called over to a group reminiscing about earlier Christmases, and presently Aunt Beatrix joined them, with Cokker close behind, bringing fresh tea. Everyone clustered around her, and Anneliese said bossily, 'I'll ring for sandwiches; Cokker should have brought them.'

Aunt Beatrix paused in her talk to say loudly, 'You'll do
nothing of the kind. If I want sandwiches, Cokker will bring
them. I dare say you mean well,' went on Aunt Beatrix tartly,
'but please remember that I am a member of the family and
familiar with the household.' She added sharply, 'Why aren't
you with Ruerd? You see little enough of each other.'

'He's doing something—he said he would have his tea
in the study.' Anneliese added self-righteously, 'I never
interfere with his work, *mevrouw*.'

Aunt Beatrix gave a well-bred snort. She said something
in Dutch which, of course, Emmy didn't understand and
which made Anneliese look uncomfortable.

Cokker returned then, set a covered dish before Aunt
Beatrix, removed the lid to reveal hot buttered toast and
then slid behind Emmy's chair. 'If you will come with me,
miss, your mother requires you.'

Emmy got up. 'There's nothing wrong?' she asked him
quietly, and he shook his head and smiled. 'You will
excuse me, *mevrouw*,' said Emmy quietly. 'My mother is
asking for me.'

She went unhurriedly from the room, following Cokker
into the hall as Aunt Beatrix, reverting to her own tongue,
said, 'There goes a girl with pretty manners. I approve of her.'

A remark tantamount, in the eyes of her family, to receiving a medal.

Cokker led the way across the hall and opened the study
door, ushered Emmy into the room and closed the door
gently behind her. The professor was there, sitting at his
desk, and her mother and father were sitting comfortably
in the two leather chairs on either side of the small fireplace, in which a brisk fire burned.

There was a tea tray beside her mother's chair and the
professor, who had stood up as Emmy went in, asked,

'You have had your tea, Ermentrude? Would you like another cup, perhaps?'

Emmy sat down composedly, her insides in a turmoil. I must learn to control my feelings, she reflected, and said briskly, 'Cokker said that Mother wanted to see me.'

'Well, yes, dear—we all do. Ruerd was telling us that his sister would like you to stay for a while and help with her children. We think it's a splendid idea but, of course, you must do what you like. Though, as Ruerd says, you really need a holiday and a change of scene, and we can get the lodge put to rights before you come back home.'

Emmy could hear the relief in her mother's voice. The prospect of getting the lodge in order while cherishing her daughter—who, according to the professor, needed a quiet and comfortable life for a few weeks—was daunting. The lodge would be cold and damp, and there were tea-chests of things to be unpacked, not to mention getting meals and household chores. Having a semi-invalid around the place would be no help at all. Much as she loved her child, Mrs Foster could be forgiven for welcoming the solving of an awkward problem.

Wasn't too much concern being expressed about her health? wondered Emmy. After all, it had only been a bang on the head, and she felt perfectly all right.

'I'll be glad to stay for a little while and help Joke with the children,' she said composedly.

'Splendid,' said the professor. 'Ermentrude will be in good hands, Mrs Foster. Cokker and Tiele will look after my sister and the children and Ermentrude. Alemke will go home directly after Christmas, and so will Aunt Beatrix and the cousins. It will be nice for Cokker to have someone in the house. Joke will be here for a couple of weeks, I believe, and I'll see that Ermentrude will have a comfortable journey home.'

He's talking just as though I wasn't here, reflected Emmy. For two pins I'd say… He smiled at her then and she found herself smiling back, quite forgetting his high-handedness.

Dinner that evening was festive. Emmy wished that she had a dress to do justice to the occasion, but the brown velvet had to pass muster once again. Anneliese, in the splendour of gold tissue and chiffon, gave her a slight smile as she entered the drawing room—much more eloquent than words.

Despite that, Emmy enjoyed herself. Tonight it was mushrooms in garlic, roast pheasant and red cabbage and a mouth-watering selection of desserts. And a delicious red wine which Emmy found very uplifting to the spirits.

Anneliese's father came to drive her home later, and Emmy felt everyone relax. It was an hour or two later before the party broke up, everyone going to their beds, in a very convivial mood. She had hardly spoken to the professor, and his goodnight was friendly and casual.

'A delightful evening,' said Mrs Foster, bidding Emmy goodnight at her bedroom door. 'Ruerd is a delightful man and a splendid host. Although I cannot see how he could possibly be in love with Anneliese. A nasty, conceited woman, if you ask me.'

'She's beautiful,' said Emmy, and kissed her mother goodnight.

Christmas Day proved to be everything it should be. After breakfast everyone, children included, loaded themselves into cars and drove to the village church, where Emmy was delighted to hear carols just as she would have expected to hear in England—only they were sung in Dutch, of course. The tunes were the same; she sang the English words and the professor, standing beside her, smiled to himself.

Lunch was a buffet, with the children on their best behaviour because once lunch was over they would all go into the hall and the presents would be handed out from under the tree, now splendidly lighted. Everyone was there—Cokker and Tiele and the housemaids and the gardener—but no Anneliese.

'She'll come this evening,' whispered Joke. She added waspishly, 'When the children are all in bed and there is no danger of sticky fingers.'

Handing out the presents took a long time; there was a great deal of unwrapping of parcels and exclamations of delight at their contents, and the children went from one to the other, showing off their gifts. There was a present for Mrs Foster, too—an evening handbag of great elegance—and for Mr Foster a box of cigars. For Emmy there was a blue cashmere scarf, the colour of a pale winter sky. It was soft and fine, and she stroked it gently. Every time she wore it, she promised herself, she would remember the professor.

Tea was noisy and cheerful but, very soon afterwards, the children—now tired and cross—were swept away to their beds. Nanny came to fetch them, looking harassed, and Emmy asked Joke if she might go with her. 'Just to help a bit,' she said diffidently.

'Oh, would you like to?' Joke beamed at her. 'Alemke has a headache, but I'll be up presently to say goodnight. You'd truly like to? I mean, don't feel that you must.'

Emmy smiled. 'I'd like to.'

She slipped away and spent the next hour under Nanny's stern eye, getting damp from splashed bathwater and warm from coaxing small, wriggling bodies into nightclothes. They were all settled at last and, with a nod

of thanks from Nanny, Emmy went back downstairs.
Everyone was dressing for dinner, she realised as she
reached the hall.

Not quite everyone; she found the professor beside her.

She turned to go back upstairs again. 'I ought to be
changing,' she said quickly. 'Thank you for my scarf. I've
never had anything cashmere before.'

He didn't say anything, but wrapped his great arms
round her and kissed her.

She was so taken by surprise that she didn't do
anything for a moment. She had no breath anyway. The
kiss hadn't been a social peck; it had lingered far too
long. And besides, she had the odd feeling that something
was alight inside her, giving her the pleasant feeling that
she could float in the air if she wished. If that was what
a kiss did to one, she thought hazily, then one must avoid
being kissed again.

She disentangled herself. 'You shouldn't...' she began.
'What I mean is, you mustn't kiss me. Anneliese
wouldn't like it...'

He was staring down at her, an odd look on his face.
'But you did, Ermentrude?'

She nodded. 'It's not fair to her,' she said, and then,
unable to help herself, asked, 'Why did you do it?'

He smiled. 'My dear Ermentrude, look up above our
heads. Mistletoe—see? A mistletoe kiss, permissible even
between the truest strangers. And really we aren't much
more than that, are we?'

He gave her an avuncular pat on the shoulder. 'Run
along and dress or you will be late for drinks.'

Emmy didn't say anything; her throat was crowded
with tears and she could feel the hot colour creeping into

her face. She flew up the staircase without a sound. Somewhere to hide, she thought unhappily. He was laughing at me.

But the professor wasn't laughing.

CHAPTER EIGHT

THERE was very little time left for Emmy to dress. Which was perhaps just as well. She lay too long in the bath and had to tear into her clothes, zipping up the brown dress with furious fingers, brushing her hair until her eyes watered.

She had made a fool of herself; the professor must have been amused, he must have seen how his kiss had affected her—like a silly schoolgirl, she told her reflection. If only she didn't love him she would hate him. She would be very cool for the entire evening, let him see that she considered his kiss—his mistletoe kiss, she reminded herself—was no consequence at all.

Her mother and father had already gone downstairs; she hurried after them just in time to see Anneliese making an entrance. Vivid peacock-blue taffeta this evening. In a style slightly too girlish for the wearer, decided Emmy waspishly, before going to greet Grandmother ter Mennolt—who had spent most of the day in her room but had now joined the family party, wearing purple velvet and a cashmere shawl fastened with the largest diamond brooch Emmy had ever set eyes on.

Emmy wished her good evening and would have moved away, but the old lady caught her arm. 'Stay, child. I have seen very little of you. I enjoyed a talk with your parents. They return tomorrow?'

'Yes, *mevrouw*. I'm staying for a little while to help Joke while her nanny goes on holiday.'

'You will be here for the New Year? It is an important occasion to us in Holland.'

'I don't know; I shouldn't think so. Will it be a family gathering again?'

'Yes, but just for the evening. You are enjoying yourself?'

'Yes, thank you. Very much.'

'Excellent. Now run along and join the others.' The old lady smiled. 'I must confess that I prefer the quiet of my room, but it is Christmas and one must make merry!'

Which described the evening very well—drinks before dinner sent everyone into the dining room full of *bonhomie*, to sit down to a traditional Christmas dinner—turkey, Christmas pudding, mince pies, crackers, port and walnuts...

The cousin sitting next to Emmy, whose name she had forgotten, accepted a second mince pie. 'Of course, not all Dutch families celebrate as we do here. This is typically English, is it not? But you see we have married into English families from time to time, and this is one of the delightful customs we have adopted. Will you be here for the New Year?'

'I don't know. I don't expect so. I'm only staying for a few days while Nanny has a holiday.'

'We return home tomorrow—all of us. But we shall be here again for New Year. But only for one night. We are that rare thing—a happy family. We enjoy meeting each other quite frequently. You have brothers and sisters?'

'No, there is just me. But I have always been happy at home.'

'The children like you...'

'Well, I like them.' She smiled at him and turned to the elderly man on her other side. She wasn't sure who he was, and his English was heavily accented, but he was, like everyone else—except Anneliese and her parents—friendly towards her.

After dinner everyone went back to the drawing room, to talk and gossip, going from group to group, and Emmy found herself swept up by Joke, listening to the lively chatter, enjoying herself and quite forgetting the brown dress and the way in which the professor avoided her.

It was while Joke, her arm linked in Emmy's, was talking to friends of the professor's—a youngish couple and something, she gathered, to do with one of the hospitals—that Anneliese joined them.

She tapped Emmy on the arm. 'Ruerd tells me you are to stay here for a few weeks as nanny to Joke's children. How fortunate you are, Emmy, to find work so easily after your lovely holiday.' She gave a titter. 'Let us hope that it hasn't given you ideas above your station.'

Emmy reminded herself that this was the professor's fiancée and that after this evening she need not, with any luck, ever see her again. Which was just as well, for the temptation to slap her was very strong.

She said in a gentle voice, aware that her companions were bating their breath, 'I'm sure you will agree with me that work at any level is preferable to idling away one's life, wasting money on unsuitable clothes—' she cast an eloquent eye at Anneliese's flat chest '—and wasting one's days doing nothing.'

If I sound like a prig, that's too bad, thought Emmy, and smiled her sweetest smile.

Now what would happen?

Joke said instantly, 'You're quite right, Emmy—I'm

sure I agree, Anneliese.' And she was backed up by murmurs from her companions.

Anneliese, red in the face, said sharply, 'Well, of course I do. Excuse me, I must speak to Aunt Beatrix…'

'You mean *our* aunt Beatrix,' said Joke in a voice of kindly reproval. Anneliese shot her a look of pure dislike and went away without another word.

'I simply must learn to hold my tongue,' said Joke, and giggled. 'I'm afraid I shall be a very nasty sister-in-law. Alemke is much more civil, although it plays havoc with her temper.'

She caught Emmy's sleeve. 'Come and talk to Grandmother. She will be going back to den Haag in the morning. Well, everyone will be going, won't they? Ruerd last of all, after lunch, and that leaves you and the children and me, Emmy.'

'I shall like that,' said Emmy. She was still shaking with rage. Anneliese would go to Ruerd and tell him how rude she had been, and he would never speak to her again…

She was talking to her mother when Anneliese went home with her parents. She gave them no more than a cool nod as she swept past them. The professor, as a good host should, saw them into their car and when he came back went to talk to his grandmother. It wasn't until everyone was dispersing much later to their beds that he came to wish the Fosters a good night and to hope that they had enjoyed their evening.

'I trust that you enjoyed yourself, too, Ermentrude,' he observed, looking down his splendid nose at her.

How nice if one could voice one's true thoughts and feelings, thought Emmy, assuring him in a polite voice that she had had a splendid evening.

He said, 'Good, good. I have to go to Leiden in the morning, but I shall see you before we go after lunch.'

For the last time, thought Emmy, and kissed her mother and father goodnight and went up the staircase to her bed.

Once breakfast was over in the morning people began to leave—stopping for a last-minute gossip, going back to find something they'd forgotten to pack, exchanging last-minute messages. They went at last, and within minutes the professor had got into his car and driven away too, leaving Emmy and her parents with Joke and the children.

Mrs Foster went away to finish her packing and Mr Foster retired to the library to read the *Daily Telegraph*, which Cokker had conjured up from somewhere. Since Joke wanted to talk to Tiele about the running of the house once the professor had gone, Emmy dressed the children in their outdoor things, wrapped herself in her coat, tied a scarf over her head and took them off to the village, with Solly and Tip for company.

They bought sweets in the small village shop and the dogs crunched the biscuits old Mevrouw Kamp offered them while she took a good look at Emmy, nodding and smiling while the children talked. Emmy had no doubt that it was about her, but the old lady looked friendly enough and, when she offered the children a sweetie from the jar on the counter, she offered Emmy one too. It tasted horrid, but she chewed it with apparent pleasure and wondered what it was.

'*Zoute* drop,' she was told. 'And weren't they delicious?'

For anyone partial to a sweet made of salt probably they were, thought Emmy, and swallowed the last morsel thankfully.

They lunched early as the professor wanted to leave by one o'clock. He joined in the talk—teasing the children, making last-minute arrangements with his sister, discussing the latest news with Mr Foster. But, although he was careful to see that Emmy had all that she wanted and was included in the talk, he had little to say to her.

I shan't see him again, thought Emmy, and I can't bear it. She brightened, though, when she remembered that she would be going back to England later and there was a chance that he might take her if he was on one of his flying visits to one or other of the hospitals. The thought cheered her so much that she was able to bid him goodbye with brisk friendliness and thank him suitably for her visit. 'It was a lovely Christmas,' she told him, and offered a hand, to have it engulfed in his.

His brief, too cheerful, 'Yes, it was, wasn't it?' made it only too plain that behind his good manners he didn't care tuppence...

She bade her mother and father goodbye, pleased to see what a lot of good these few days had done them. A little luxury never harmed anyone, she reflected, and hoped that the lodge would be quickly restored to normal.

'When you get home everything will be sorted out,' her mother assured her. 'Your father and I feel so rested we can tackle anything. Take care of yourself, love, won't you? Ruerd says you could do with a few more days before you go job-hunting.'

If it hadn't been for the children the house would have seemed very quiet once its master had driven away, but the rest of the day was taken up with the pleasurable task of re-examining the presents which they had had at Christmas, and a visit to the village shop once more to buy paper and envelopes for the less pleasurable task of writing the thank-you letters.

On the following day they all got into Joke's car and drove along the coast as far as Alkmaar. The cheese museum was closed for the winter, but there was the clock, with its mechanical figures circling round it on each hour, and the lovely cathedral church, as well as the picturesque old houses and shops. They lunched in a small café, off *erwtensoep*—a pea soup so thick that a spoon could stand upright in it—and *roggebrood*. The children made Emmy repeat the names after them, rolling around with laughter at her efforts.

It was a surprisingly happy day, and Emmy was kept too busy to think about the professor. Only that night as she got into bed did she spare him a thought. He would be back in Chelsea by now, with Beaker looking after him. He would have phoned Anneliese, of course. He would miss her, thought Emmy sleepily, although how a man could miss anyone as disagreeable as she was a bit of a puzzle.

There was a phone call from her mother in the morning. They had had a splendid trip back; Ruerd had taken them right to their door, and there had been a letter waiting for them, telling them that the furniture would be removed in a day's time.

'So now we can get things straight,' said her mother happily. 'And Ruerd is so splendid—he unloaded a box of the most delicious food for us, and a bottle of champagne. One meets such a person so seldom in life, and when one does it is so often for a brief period. We shall miss him. He sent his kind regards, by the way, love.'

An empty, meaningless phrase, reflected Emmy.

She was to have the children all day as Joke was going to den Haag to the hairdresser's and to do some shopping. It was a bright, cold day, so, with everyone well wrapped-up, she led them down to the sea, tramping along the sand with Tip and Solly gavotting around them. They all threw sticks, racing up and down, shouting and laughing to each other, playing tig, daring each other to run to the water's edge and back.

Emmy shouted with them; there was no one else to hear or see them, and the air was exhilarating. They trooped back presently, tired and hungry, to eat the lunch Cokker had waiting for them and then go to the nursery, where they sat around the table playing cards—the littlest one on Emmy's lap, her head tucked into Emmy's shoulder, half asleep.

They had tea there presently and, since Joke wasn't back yet, Emmy set about getting them ready for bed. Bathed and clad in dressing gowns they were eating their suppers when their mother returned.

'Emmy, you must be worn out. I never meant to be so long, but I met some friends and had lunch with them and then I had the shopping to do. Have you hated it?'

'I've enjoyed every minute,' said Emmy quite truth-fully. 'I had a lovely day; I only hope the children did, too.'

'Well, tomorrow we're all going to den Haag to have lunch with my mother and father. They were away for Christmas—in Denmark with a widowed aunt. They'll be here for New Year, though. You did know that we had parents living?'

'The professor mentioned it.'

'Christmas wasn't quite the same without them, but we'll all be here in a few days.'

'You want me to come with you tomorrow?' asked Emmy. 'I'm quite happy to stay here—I mean, it's family…'

Joke smiled. 'I want you to come if you will, Emmy.' She wondered if she should tell her that her parents had been told all about her by Ruerd, and decided not to. It was his business. They had never been a family to interfere with each other's lives, although she and Alemke very much wished to dissuade him from marrying Anneliese.

There was undoubtedly something Ruerd was keeping to himself, and neither of them had seen any sign of love or even affection in his manner towards Anneliese, although he was attentive to her needs and always concerned for her comfort. Good manners wouldn't allow him to be otherwise. And he had been careful to avoid being alone with Emmy at Christmas. Always polite towards her, his friendliness also aloof. Knowing her brother, Joke knew that he wouldn't break his word to Anneliese, although she strongly suspected that he had more than a casual interest in Emmy.

They drove to den Haag in good spirits in the morning. The children spoke a little English and Emmy taught them some of the old-fashioned nursery rhymes, which they sang for most of the way. Only as they reached a long, stately avenue with large houses on each side of it did Emmy suggest that they should stop. Joke drove up the short drive of one of these houses and stopped before its ponderous door. 'Well, here we are,' she declared. 'Oma and Opa will be waiting.'

The door opened as they reached it and a stout, elderly woman welcomed them.

'This is Nynke,' said Joke, and Emmy shook hands and waited while the children hugged and kissed her. 'The housekeeper. She has been with us since I was a little girl.' It was her turn to be hugged and kissed before they all went into the hall to take off coats and scarves and gloves, and go through the arched double doors Nynke was holding open for them.

The elderly couple waiting for them at the end of the long, narrow room made an imposing pair. The professor's parents were tall—his father with the massive frame he had passed on to his son, and his mother an imposing, rather stout figure. They both had grey hair, and his father was still a handsome man, but his mother, despite her elegant bearing, had a homely face, spared from downright plainness by a pair of very blue eyes.

No wonder he has fallen in love with Anneliese, reflected Emmy, with that lovely face and golden hair.

The children swarmed over their grandparents, although they were careful to mind their manners, and presently stood quietly while Joke greeted her parents.

'And this is Emmy,' she said, and put a hand on Emmy's arm. 'I am so glad to have her with me for a few days—she's been staying with her parents over Christmas at Huis ter Mennolt. Rik's away, and it's lovely to have company.'

Emmy shook hands, warmed by friendly smiles and greetings in almost accentless English. Presently Mevrouw ter Mennolt drew her to one side and, over coffee and tiny almond biscuits, begged her to tell her something of herself.

'Ruerd mentioned that he had guests from England when he phoned us. You know him well?'

The nice, plain face smiled, the blue eyes twinkled. Emmy embarked on a brief résumé of her acquaintance with the professor, happily unaware that her companion had already had a detailed account from her son. It was what he *hadn't* said which had convinced his mother that he was more than a little interested in Emmy.

Watching Emmy's face, almost as plain as her own, she wished heartily for a miracle before Anneliese managed to get her son to the altar. Mevrouw ter Mennolt had tried hard to like her, since her son was to marry the girl, but she had had no success, and Anneliese, confident in her beauty and charm, had never made an effort to gain her future mother-in-law's affection.

Emmy would, however, do very nicely. Joke had told her that she was right for Ruerd, and she found herself agreeing.

The children liked her and that, for a doting grandmother, was an important point. She hadn't forgotten Anneliese once flying into a rage during a visit because Joke's youngest had accidentally put a grubby little paw on Anneliese's white skirt. It was a pity that Ruerd hadn't been there, for her lovely face had grown ugly with temper. Besides, this quiet, rather shabbily dressed girl might be the one woman in the world who understood Ruerd, a man who's feelings ran deep and hidden from all but those who loved him.

Emmy was handed over to her host presently, and although she was at first wary of this older edition of the professor he put her at her ease in minutes, talking about gardening, dogs and cats, and presently he bade her fetch her coat.

'We have a garden here,' he told her. 'Not as splendid as that at Huis ter Mennolt, but sufficient for us and Max. Let us take the dogs for a quick run before lunch.'

They went through the house, into a conservatory, out of doors onto a terrace and down some steps to the garden below. Max, the black Labrador, Solly and Tip went with them, going off the path to search for imaginary rabbits, while Emmy and Ruerd's father walked briskly down its considerable length to the shrubbery at the end.

All the while they talked. At least, the old man talked, and a great deal of what he said concerned his son. Emmy learned more about Ruerd in fifteen minutes than she had in all the weeks she had known him. She listened avidly; soon she would never see him again, so every small scrap of information about him was precious, to be stored away, to be mulled over in a future empty of him.

Back at the house she led the children away to have their hands washed and their hair combed before lunch. They went up the stairs and into one of the bathrooms—old-fashioned like the rest of the house, but lacking nothing in comfort. She liked the house. It wasn't like Huis ter Mennolt; it had been built at a later date—mid-nineteenth century, she guessed—and the furniture was solid and beautifully cared for. Beidermeier? she thought, not knowing much about it. Its walls were hung with family portraits and she longed to study them as she urged the children downstairs once again, all talking at once and laughing at her attempts to understand them.

She was offered dry sherry in the drawing room while the children drank something pink and fizzy—a special drink they always had at their grandmother's, they told her, before they all went into the dining room for lunch.

It was a pleasant meal, with the children on their best behaviour and conversation which went well with eating the lamb chops which followed the celery soup—nothing deep which required long pauses while something was debated and explained—and nothing personal. No one, thought Emmy, had mentioned Anneliese once, which, since she was so soon to be a member of the family, seemed strange.

Christmas was discussed, and plans for the New Year.

'We shall all meet again at Huis ter Mennolt,' explained Joke. 'Just for dinner in the evening, and to wish each other a happy New Year. Ruerd will come back just for a day or two; he never misses.'

They sat around after lunch, and presently, when the children became restive, Emmy sat them round a table at the other end of the drawing room and suggested cards. 'Snap', 'beggar your neighbour' and 'beat your neighbour out of doors' she had already taught them, and they settled down to play. Presently she was making as much noise as they were.

It was a large room; the three persons at the other end of it were able to talk without hindrance, and, even if Emmy could have heard them, she couldn't have understood a word. Good manners required them to talk in English while she was with them, but now they embarked on the subject nearest to their hearts—Ruerd.

They would have been much cheered if they had known that he was in his office at St Luke's, sitting at his desk piled with patients' notes, charts and department reports, none of which he was reading. He was thinking about Emmy.

When he returned to Holland in a few days' time, he would ask Anneliese to release him from their engagement. It was a step he was reluctant to take for, although he had no feeling for her any more, he had no wish to humiliate her with her friends. But to marry her when he loved Ermentrude was out of the question. Supposing Ermentrude wouldn't have him? He smiled a little; then he would have to remain a bachelor for the rest of his days.

He would have his lovely home in Holland, his pleasant house in Chelsea, his dogs, his work…but a bleak prospect without her.

Joke, Emmy and the children drove back to Huis ter Mennolt after tea. With the coming of evening it was much colder. 'We shall probably have some snow before much longer,' said Joke. 'Do you skate, Emmy?'

'No, only roller-skating when I was a little girl. We don't get much snow at home.'

'Well, we can teach you while you are here.' Joke added quickly, 'Nanny isn't coming back for another couple of days. Her mother has the flu, and she doesn't want to give it to the children. You won't mind staying for a few days longer?'

Emmy didn't mind. She didn't mind where she was if the professor wasn't going to be there too.

'You've heard from your mother?' asked Joke.

'Yes; everything is going very well at last. The furniture will be gone today and the plumber has almost finished whatever it was he had to do. By the time the term starts they should be well settled in. I ought to have been there to help…'

'Well, Ruerd advised against it, didn't he? And I dare say your mother would have worried over you if you had worked too hard or got wet.'

'Well, yes, I suppose so.'

Emmy eased the smallest child onto her lap so that Solly could lean against her shoulder. Tip was in front with the eldest boy. It was a bit of a squash in the big car, but it was warm and comfortable, smelling of damp dog and the peppermints the children were eating.

The next morning Joke went back to den Haag. 'Cokker will look after you all,' she told Emmy. 'Take the children out if you like. They're getting excited about New Year. Everyone will be coming tomorrow in time for lunch, but Ruerd phoned to say he won't get here until the evening. I hope he'll stay for a few days this time. He'll take you back with him when he does go. If that suits you?' Joke studied Emmy's face. 'You do feel better for the change? I haven't asked you to do too much?'

'I've loved every minute,' said Emmy truthfully. 'I like the children and I love this house and the seashore, and you've all been so kind to me and Mother and Father.'

'You must come and see us again,' said Joke, and looked at Emmy to see how she felt about that.

'I expect I shall have a job, but it's kind of you to invite me.'

'Ruerd could always bring you over when he comes,' persisted Joke.

'Well, I don't suppose we shall see each other. I mean, he's in London and I'll be in Dorset.'

'Will you mind that?' said Joke.

Emmy bent over the French knitting she was fixing for one of the girls.

'Yes. The professor has helped me so often—you know, when things have happened. He—he always seemed to be there, if you see what I mean. I shall always be grateful to him.'

Joke said airily, 'Yes, coincidence is a strange thing, isn't it? Some people call it fate. Well, I'm off. Ask Cokker or Tiele for anything you want. I'll try and be back in time for tea, but if the traffic's heavy I may be a bit late.'

The day was much as other days—going down to the seashore, running races on the sand, with Emmy carrying the youngest, joining in the shouting and laughing and then going back to piping hot soup and *crokettes*, and, since it was almost new year, *poffertjes*—tiny pancakes sprinkled with sugar.

The two smallest children were led upstairs to rest then, and the other two went to the billiard room where they were allowed to play snooker on the small table at one end of the room.

Which left Emmy with an hour or so to herself. She went back to the drawing room and began a slow round of the portraits and then a careful study of the contents of the two great display cabinets on either side of the fireplace. She was admiring a group of figurines—Meissen, she thought—when Cokker came into the room.

'Juffrouw van Moule has called,' he told her. 'I have said that *mevrouw* is out, but she wishes to see you, miss.'

'Me? Whatever for?' asked Emmy. 'I expect I'd better see her, hadn't I, Cokker? I don't expect she'll stay, do you?

But if the children want anything, could you please ask Tiele to go to them?'

'Yes, miss, and you will ring if you want me?'

'Thank you, Cokker.'

Anneliese came into the room with the self-assurance of someone who knew that she looked perfection itself. Indeed she was beautiful, wrapped in a soft blue wool coat, with a high-crowned Melusine hat perched on her fair hair. She took the coat off and tossed it onto a chair, sent gloves and handbag after it and sat down in one of the small easy chairs.

'Still here, Ermentrude.' It wasn't a question but a statement. 'Hanging on until the last minute. Not that it will do you any good. Ruerd must be heartily tired of you, but that is what happens when one does a good deed—one is condemned to repeat it unendingly. Still, you have had a splendid holiday, have you not? He intends that you should return to England directly after New Year. He will be staying on here for a time; we have the wedding arrangements to complete. You did know that we are to marry in January?'

She looked at Emmy's face. 'No, I see that you did not know. I expect he knew that I would tell you. So much easier for me to do it, is it not? It is embarrassing for him, knowing that you are in love with him, although heaven knows he has never given you the least encouragement. I suppose someone like you, living such a dull life, has to make do with daydreams.'

Anneliese smiled and sat back in her chair.

'It seems to me,' said Emmy, in a voice she willed to keep steady, 'that you are talking a great deal of nonsense. Is that why you came? And you haven't told me anything new. I know that you and the professor are to be married, and I know that I am going back to England as soon as

Nanny is back, and I know that you have been very rude and rather spiteful.'

She watched with satisfaction as Anneliese flushed brightly. 'I believe in being outspoken too. We dislike each other; I have no use for girls like you. Go back to England and find some clerk or shopkeeper to marry you. It is a pity that you ever had a taste of our kind of life.' She eyed Emmy shrewdly. 'You do believe me, don't you, about our marriage?'

And when Emmy didn't answer she said, 'I'll prove it.'

She got up and went to the phone on one of the side-tables. 'Ruerd's house number,' she said over her shoulder. 'If he isn't there I will ring the hospital.' She began to dial. 'And you know what I shall say? I shall tell him that you don't believe me, that you hope in your heart that he loves you and that you will continue to pester him and try and spoil his happiness.'

'You don't need to phone,' said Emmy quietly. 'I didn't believe you, but perhaps there is truth in what you say. I shall go back to England as soon as I can and I shan't see him again.'

Anneliese came back to her chair. 'And you'll say nothing when he comes here tomorrow? A pity you have to be here, but it can't be helped. Luckily there will be a number of people here; he won't have time to talk to you.'

'He never has talked to me,' said Emmy. 'Only as a guest.' Emmy got up. 'I expect you would like to go now. I don't know why you have thought of me as a—well, a rival, I suppose. You're beautiful, and I'm sure you will make the professor a most suitable wife. I hope you will both be happy.'

The words had almost choked her, but she had said them. Anneliese looked surprised, but she got into her coat, picked up her gloves and bag and went out of the room without another word. Cokker appeared a minute later.

'I have prepared a pot of tea, miss; I am sure you would enjoy it.'

Emmy managed a smile. 'Oh, Cokker, thank you. I'd love it.'

He came with the tray and set it down beside her chair. 'The English, I understand, drink tea at any time, but especially at moments of great joy or despair.'

'Yes, Cokker, you are quite right; they do.'

She wasn't going to cry, she told herself, drinking the hot tea, forcing it down over the lump of tears in her throat.

She tried not to think about the things Anneliese had said. They had been spiteful, but they had had the ring of truth. Had she been so transparent in her feelings towards Ruerd? She had thought—and how silly and stupid she had been—that his kiss under the mistletoe had meant something. She didn't know what, but it had been like a spark between them. Perhaps Anneliese was right and she had been allowing herself to daydream.

Emmy went pale at the thought of meeting him, but she had the rest of the day and most of tomorrow in which to pull herself together, and the first chance she got she would go back to England.

The children had their tea and she began on the leisurely task of getting them to bed after a rousing game of ludo. They were in their dressing gowns and eating their suppers when Joke got back, and it wasn't until she and Emmy had dined that Emmy asked her when Nanny would be coming back.

'You are not happy. I have given you too much to do—the children all day long...'

'No, no. I love it here and I like being with the children,

only I think that I should go home as soon as Nanny comes back. I don't mean to sound ungrateful—it's been like a lovely holiday—but I must start looking for a job.'

Emmy spoke briskly but her face was sad, and Joke wondered why. She had her answer as Emmy went on in a determinedly cheerful voice, 'Anneliese called this afternoon. I should have told you sooner, but there were so many other things to talk about with the children. She only stayed for a few minutes.'

'Why did she come here? What did she say?'

'Nothing, really; she just sort of popped in. She didn't leave any messages for you. Perhaps she wanted to know something to do with tomorrow. She will be coming, of course.'

'Oh, yes, she will be here. Was she civil? She doesn't like you much, does she?'

'No; I don't know why. She was quite polite.'

I could tell you why, thought Joke—you've stolen Ruerd's heart, something Anneliese knows she can never do.

She said aloud, 'Nanny phoned this evening while you were getting the children into bed. She will be back the day after tomorrow. I hate to see you go, Emmy.'

'I shan't forget any of you, or this house and the people in it,' said Emmy.

She had no time to think about her own plans. The house was in a bustle, getting ready for the guests. Tiele was in the kitchen making piles of *oliebolljes*—a kind of doughnut which everyone ate at New Year—and the maids were hurrying here and there, laying the table for a buffet lunch and getting a guest room ready in case Grandmother ter Mennolt should need to rest.

'She never misses,' said Joke. 'She and Aunt Beatrix live

together at Wassenaar—that's a suburb of den Haag. They
have a housekeeper and Jon, the chauffeur, who sees to the
garden and stokes the boiler and so on. The aunts and
uncles and cousins you met at Christmas will come—oh,
and Anneliese, of course.'

Almost everyone came for lunch, although guests were
still arriving during the afternoon. Anneliese had arrived
for lunch, behaving, as Joke said sourly, as though she
were already the mistress of the house. Her parents were
with her, and a youngish man whom she introduced as an
old friend who had recently returned to Holland.

'We lost touch,' she explained. 'We were quite close…'
She smiled charmingly and he put an arm round her waist
and smiled down at her. She had spoken in Dutch, and
Alemke had whispered a translation in Emmy's ear.

'How dare she bring that man here?' she added. 'And
Ruerd won't be here until quite late this evening… Oh, how
I wish something would happen…'

Sometimes a wish is granted. The professor, by dint of
working twice as hard as usual, was ready to leave Chelsea
by the late morning. Seen off by Beaker and Charlie, he
drove to Dover, crossed over the channel and made good
time to his house. It was dark when he arrived, and the
windows were ablaze. He let himself in through a side door,
pleased to be home, and even more pleased at the thought
of seeing Emmy again. He walked along the curved passage
behind the hall and then paused at a half-open door of a
small sitting room, seldom used. Whoever was there
sounded like Anneliese. He opened the door and went in.

CHAPTER NINE

T WAS indeed Anneliese, in the arms of a man the professor didn't know, being kissed and kissing with unmistakable ardour.

With such ardour that they didn't see him. He stood in the doorway, watching them, until the man caught sight of him, pushed Anneliese away and then caught her hand in his.

The professor strolled into the room. 'I don't think I have had the pleasure of meeting you,' he said pleasantly. 'Anneliese, please introduce me to your friend.'

Anneliese was for once at a loss for words. The man held out a hand. 'Hubold Koppelar, an old friend of Anneliese.'

The professor ignored the hand. He looked down his splendid nose at Koppelar. 'How old?' he asked. 'Before Anneliese became engaged to me?'

Anneliese had found her tongue. 'Of course it was. Hubold went away to Canada; I thought he would never come back...'

The professor took out his spectacles, put them on and looked at her carefully. 'So you made do with me?'

Anneliese tossed her head. 'Well, what else was there to do? I want a home and money, like any other woman.'

'I am now no longer necessary to your plans for the future, though?' asked the professor gently. 'Consider yourself free, Anneliese, if that is what you want.'

Hubold drew her hand through his arm. 'She wants it all right. Of course, we hadn't meant it to be like this—we would have let you down lightly...'

The professor's eyes were like flint, but he smiled. 'Very good of you. And now the matter is settled there is no need for us to meet again, is there? I regret that I cannot show you the door at this moment, but the New Year is an occasion in this house and I won't have it spoilt. I must ask you both to remain and behave normally until after midnight. Now, let us go together and meet my guests...'

So Emmy, about to go upstairs to get into the despised brown dress, was one of the first to see him come into the hall, with Anneliese on one side of him and the man she had brought with her on the other. It was easy to escape for everyone else surged forward to meet him.

'Ruerd, how lovely,' cried Joke. 'We didn't expect you until much later...'

'An unexpected surprise,' said the professor, and watched Emmy's small person disappear up the staircase. Nothing of his feelings showed on his face.

He made some laughing remark to Anneliese and went to talk to his grandmother and father and mother, then presently to mingle with his guests before everyone went away to change for the evening.

Emmy didn't waste much time on dressing. She took a uninterested look at her person in the looking-glass, put a few extra pins into the coil of hair in the nape of her neck and went along to the nursery to make sure that the children were ready for bed. As a great treat, they were to be roused just before midnight and brought downstairs to greet the New Year, on the understanding that they went to their beds punctually and went to sleep.

It seemed unlikely that they would, thought Emmy, tucking them in while she wondered how best to arrange her departure just as soon as possible.

To travel on New Year's Day would be impossible, but if she could see the professor in the morning and ask him to arrange for her to travel on the following day she would only need to stay one more day. And with so many people in the house it would be easy enough to keep out of the way. Anyway, he would surely be wrapped up in Anneliese. Emmy would get up early and pack, just in case there was some way of leaving sooner.

Fortune smiled on her for once. Sitting in a quiet corner of the drawing room was Oom Domus, middle-aged and a widower. He told her that he was going to the Hook of Holland to catch the ferry to England late on New Year's Day. 'It sails at midnight, as you may know. There will be almost no trains and buses or ferries tomorrow. It is very much a national holiday here.'

'Do you drive there?' asked Emmy.

'Yes; I'm going to stay with friends in Warwickshire.'

Emmy took a quick breath. 'Would you mind very much giving me a lift as far as Dover? I'm going back to England now that Nanny will be back tomorrow.'

If Oom Domus was surprised he didn't show it. 'My dear young lady, I shall be delighted. You live in Dorset, do you not? Far better if I drive you on to London and drop you off at whichever station you want.'

'You're very kind. I—I haven't seen the professor to tell him yet, but I'm sure he won't mind.'

Oom Domus had watched Ruerd not looking at Emmy,

just as she was careful not to look at him. He thought it likely that both of them would mind, but he wasn't going to say so. He said easily, 'I shall leave around seven o'clock tomorrow evening, my dear. That will give you plenty of time to enjoy your day.'

As far as Emmy was concerned the day was going to be far too long. She wanted to get away as quickly as she could, away from Ruerd and his lovely home, and away from Anneliese.

Aunt Beatrix joined them then, and Emmy looked around her at the laughing and talking people near her. There was no sign of the professor for the moment, but Anneliese was there, as beautiful as ever, in yards of trailing chiffon. She was laughing a great deal, and looked flushed. Excitement at seeing Ruerd again? Or drinking too much?

Emmy took a second glass of sherry when Cokker offered it; perhaps if she drank everything she was offered during the evening it would be over more quickly. She caught sight of the professor's handsome features as he came across the room; she tossed back the sherry and beat a retreat into a group of cousins, who smilingly welcomed her and switched to English as easily as changing hats.

If the professor had noticed this, he gave no sign, merely passed the time of day with his uncle and went to talk to Joke.

'You look like a cat who's swallowed the cream,' she told him. 'What's going on behind that bland face of yours?'

When he only smiled she said, 'Nanny's back tomorrow. Have you arranged to take Emmy home?'

'No, not yet.'

'For some reason she's keen to go as soon as possible— said she has to find a job.'

'I'll talk to her when there's a quiet moment. Here's Cokker to tell us that dinner is served.'

Twenty persons sat down to the table which had been extended for the occasion, and Emmy found herself between two of the professor's friends—pleasant, middle-aged men who knew England well and kept up a lively conversation throughout the meal.

Emmy, very slightly muzzy from her tossed-back sherry, ate her mushrooms in garlic and cream, drank a glass of white wine with the lobster Thermidor and a glass of red wine with the kidneys in a calvados and cream sauce. And another glass of sweet white wine with the trifle and mince pies...

The meal was leisurely and the talk lively. The professor's father, sitting at the head of the table, listened gravely to Anneliese, who was so animated that Emmy decided that she really had drunk too much. Like me, reflected Emmy uneasily. He had Grandmother ter Mennolt on his other side, who, excepting when good manners demanded, ignored Anneliese. The professor was at the other end of the table, sitting beside his mother with Aunt Beatrix on his other side. Emmy wondered why he and Anneliese weren't sitting together. Perhaps there was a precedent about these occasions...

They had coffee at the table so that it was well after eleven o'clock before everyone went back to the drawing room. Anneliese was with Ruerd now, her friend at the other end of the room talking to Joke's husband. Emmy wondered if the professor would make some sort of announcement about his forthcoming marriage; Anneliese had told her that it was to be within the next few weeks, and presumably everyone there would be invited.

Nothing was said, and just before twelve o'clock she slipped away to rouse the children and bring them down to the drawing room. The older ones were awake—she suspected that they hadn't been to sleep yet—but the smaller ones needed a good deal of rousing. She was joined by Joke and Alemke presently, and they led the children downstairs, where they stood, owl-eyed and excited, each with a small glass of lemonade with which to greet the New Year.

Someone had tuned into the BBC, and Cokker was going round filling glasses with champagne. The maids and the gardener had joined them by now, and there was a ripple of excitement as Big Ben struck the first stroke. There were cries of *Gelukkige Niewe Jaar!* and the children screamed with delight as the first of the fireworks outside the drawing-room windows were set off.

Everyone was darting to and fro, kissing and shaking hands and wishing each other good luck and happiness. Emmy was kissed and greeted too, standing a little to one side with the smallest child—already half-asleep again despite the fireworks—tucked against her shoulder. Even Anneliese paused by her, but not to wish her well. All she said was, 'Tomorrow you will be back in England.'

Hubold Koppelar, circling the group, paused by her, looked her over and went past her without a word. He wasn't sure who she was; one of the maids, he supposed, detailed to look after the children. Anneliese would tell him later. For the moment they were keeping prudently apart, mindful of the professor's words, uttered so quietly but not to be ignored.

Emmy had been edging round the room, avoiding the professor as he went from one group to the other, exchanging greetings, but he finally caught up with her. She held out a hand and said stiffly, looking no higher than his tie, 'A happy New Year, Professor.'

He took the hand and held it fast. 'Don't worry, Ermentrude. I'm not going to kiss you; not here and now.'

He smiled down at her and her heart turned over.

'We shall have a chance to talk tomorrow morning,' he told her. 'Or perhaps presently, when the children are back in bed.'

Emmy gazed at him, quite unable to think of anything to say, looking so sad that he started to ask her what was the matter—to be interrupted by Aunt Beatrix, asking him briskly if he would have a word with his grandmother.

He let Emmy's hand go at last. 'Later,' he said, and smiled with such tenderness that she swallowed tears.

She watched his massive back disappear amongst his guests. He was letting her down lightly, letting her see that he was going to ignore a situation embarrassing to them both. She felt hot all over at the thought.

It was a relief to escape with the children and put them back into their beds. She wouldn't be missed, and although there was a buffet supper she couldn't have swallowed a morsel. She went to her room, undressed and got into bed, lying awake until long after the house was quiet.

There was no one at breakfast when she went downstairs in the morning. Cokker brought her coffee and toast, which she didn't want. Later, she promised herself, when the professor had a few minutes to spare, she would explain about going back to England with Oom Domus. He would be pleased; it made a neat end to an awkward situation. Anneliese would have got her way, too... She hadn't seen Anneliese after those few words; she supposed that she was spending the night here and would probably stay on now the professor was home.

Emmy got up and went to look out of the window. Ruerd was coming towards the house with Tip and Solly, coming from the direction of the shore. If she had the chance she would go once more just to watch the wintry North Sea and then walk back over the dunes along the path which would afford her a glimpse of the house beyond the garden. It was something she wanted to remember for always.

She went back upstairs before he reached the house; the children must be wakened and urged to dress and clean their teeth. Joke had said that they would be leaving that afternoon at the same time as Alemke and her husband and children.

'Everyone else will go before lunch,' she had told Emmy. 'My mother and father will stay for lunch, of course, but Grandmother and Aunt Beatrix will go at the same time as the others.'

Cousins and aunts and uncles and family and friends began to take their leave soon after breakfast, and, once they had gone, Emmy suggested that she should take the children down for a last scamper on the sands.

'Oh, would you?' asked Joke. 'Just for an hour, so they can let off steam? Nanny will be waiting for us when we get home. They're going to miss you, Emmy.'

The professor was in his study with his father. Emmy bundled the children into their coats, wrapped herself up against the winter weather outside and hurried them away before he should return. She still had to tell him that she was leaving, but perhaps a brisk run out of doors would give her the courage to do so.

At the end of an hour, she marshalled her charges into some sort of order and went back to the house, and, since their boots and shoes were covered in damp sand and frost, they went in through the side door. It wasn't until it was too late to retreat that she saw the professor standing there, holding the door open.

The children milled around him, chattering like magpies, but presently he said something to them and they trooped away, leaving Emmy without a backward glance. She did her best to slide past the professor's bulk.

'I'll just go and help the children,' she began. And then went on ashamed of her cowardice, 'I wanted to see you, Professor. I'd like to go back to England today, if you don't mind. Oom Domus said he would give me a lift this evening.' When he said nothing she added, 'I've had a lovely time here, and you've been so kind. I'm very grateful, but it's time I went back to England.'

He glanced at her and looked away. 'Stay a few more days, Ermentrude. I'll take you back when I go.'

'I'd like to go today—and it's so convenient, isn't it? I mean, Oom Domus is going over to England this evening.'

'You have no wish to stay?' he asked, in what she thought was a very casual voice. 'We must talk…'

'No—no. I'd like to go as soon as possible.'

'By all means go with Oom Domus.' He stood aside. 'Don't let me keep you; I expect that you have things to do. Lunch will be in half an hour or so.'

She slipped past him, and then stopped as he said, without turning round, 'You have avoided me, Ermentrude. You have a reason?'

'Yes, but I don't want to talk about it. It's—personal.' She paused. 'It's something I'd rather not talk about,' she repeated.

When he didn't answer, she went away. It hadn't been at all satisfactory; she had expected him to be relieved, even if he expressed polite regret at her sudden departure. He had sounded withdrawn, as though it didn't matter whether she came or went. Probably it *didn't* matter, she told herself firmly. He must surely be relieved to bring to an end what could only have been an embarrassing episode. As for the kiss, what to her had been a glorious moment in her life had surely been a mere passing incident in his.

She went to her room and sat down to think about it. She could, of course, write to him, but what would be the point? He would think that she was wishful of continuing their friendship—had it been friendship? She no longer knew—and that would be the last thing he would want with his marriage to Anneliese imminent. Best leave things as they were, she decided, and tidied her hair, looked rather despairingly at her pale face and went down to lunch.

She had been dreading that, but there was no need. The professor offered her sherry with easy friendliness and during lunch kept the conversation to light-hearted topics, never once touching on her departure. It seemed to her that he was no longer interested in it.

She made the excuse that she still had some last-minute packing to do after lunch. If she remained in the drawing room it would mean that everyone would have to speak in English, and it was quite likely they wanted to discuss family matters in their own language. It had surprised her that Anneliese hadn't come to lunch—perhaps Ruerd was going to her home later that day. Everyone would be gone by the late afternoon and he would be able to do as he pleased.

Of course, she had no packing to do. She went and sat by the window and stared out at the garden and the dunes and the sea beyond. It would be dark in a few hours, but the sun had struggled through the clouds now, and the pale sunlight warmed the bare trees and turned the dull-grey sea into silver. It wouldn't last long; there were clouds banking up on the horizon, and a bitter wind.

She was turning away from the window when she saw the professor with his dogs, striding down the garden and across the dunes. He was bare-headed, but wearing his sheepskin jacket so that he looked even larger than he was.

She watched him for a moment, and then on an impulse

put on her own coat, tied a scarf over her head and went quietly downstairs and out of the side door. The wind took her breath as she started down the long garden, intent on reaching Ruerd while she still had the courage. She was going away, but she had given him no reason and he was entitled to that, and out here in the bleakness of the seashore it would be easier to tell him.

The wind was coming off the sea and she found it slow going; the dunes were narrow here, but they were slippery—full of hollows and unexpected hillocks. By the time she reached the sands the professor was standing by the water, watching the waves tumbling towards him.

The sun had gone again. She walked towards him, soundless on the sand, and when she reached him put out a hand and touched his sleeve.

He turned and looked at her then, and she saw how grim he looked and how tired. She forgot her speech for a moment.

'You ought not to be out in this weather without a hat,' she told him. And then, 'I can't go away without telling you why I'm going, Ruerd. I wasn't going to—Anneliese asked me not to say anything—but perhaps she won't mind if you explain to her... I'm going because I'm in love with you. You know that, don't you? She told me so. I'm sorry you found out; I didn't think it showed. It must have been awkward for you.'

She looked away from him. 'You do see that I had to tell you? But now that I have you can forget all about it. You've been kind. More than kind.' She gulped. 'I'm sure you will be very happy with Anneliese...'

If she had intended to say anything more she was given no opportunity to do so. Wrapped so tightly in his arms that she could hardly breathe she heard his voice roaring above the noise of the wind and waves.

'Kind? Kind? My darling girl, I have not been kind. I have been in love with you since the moment I first saw you, spending hours thinking up ways of seeing more of you and knowing that I had given Anneliese my promise to marry her. It has been something unbearable I never wish to live through again.'

He bent his head and kissed her. It was even better than the kiss under the mistletoe, and highly satisfactory. All the same, Emmy muttered, 'Anneliese…?'

'Anneliese no longer wishes to marry me. Forget her, my darling, and listen to me. We shall marry, you and I, and live happily ever after. You do believe that?'

Emmy peeped up into his face, no longer grim and tired but full of tenderness and love. She nodded. 'Yes, Ruerd. Oh, yes. But what about Anneliese?'

He kissed her soundly. 'We will talk later; I'm going to kiss you again.'

'Very well,' said Emmy. 'I don't mind if you do.'

They stood, the pair of them, just for a while in their own world, oblivious of the wind and the waves and the dogs running to and fro.

Heaven, thought Emmy happily, isn't necessarily sunshine and blue skies—and she reached up to put her arms round her professor's neck.

At the end of the garden, Oom Domus, coming to look for her, adjusted his binoculars, took a good look and hurried back to the house. He would have a lonely trip to England, but what did that matter? He was bursting with good news.

* * * * *

Celebrate 60 years of pure
reading pleasure with Harlequin®!
Just in time for the holidays,
Silhouette Special Edition® is proud to present
New York Times *bestselling author*
Kathleen Eagle's
ONE COWBOY, ONE CHRISTMAS

Rodeo rider Zach Beaudry was a travelin' man—
until he broke down in middle-of-nowhere South
Dakota during a deep freeze. That's when an angel
came to his rescue....

"Don't die on me. Come on, Zel. You know how much I love you, girl. You're all I've got. Don't do this to me here. Not *now*."

But Zelda had quit on him, and Zach Beaudry had no one to blame but himself. He'd taken his sweet time hitting the road, and then miscalculated a shortcut. For all he knew he was a hundred miles from gas. But even if they were sitting next to a pump, the ten dollars he had in his pocket wouldn't get him out of South Dakota, which was not where he wanted to be right now. Not even his beloved pickup truck, Zelda, could get him much of anywhere on fumes. He was sitting out in the cold in the middle of nowhere. And getting colder.

He shifted the pickup into Neutral and pulled hard on the steering wheel, using the downhill slope to get her off the blacktop and into the roadside grass, where she shuddered to a standstill. He stroked the padded dash. "You'll be safe here."

But Zach would not. It was getting dark, and it was already too damn cold for his cowboy ass. Zach's battered body was a barometer, and he was feeling South Dakota, big time. He'd have given his right arm to be climbing into a hotel hot tub instead of a brutal blast of north wind. The right was his free arm anyway. Damn thing had lost altitude, touched some part of the bull and caused him a scoreless ride last time out.

It wasn't scoring him a ride this night, either. A carload of teenagers whizzed by, topping off the insult by laying on the horn as they passed him. It was at least twenty minutes before another vehicle came along. He stepped out and waved both arms this time, damn near getting himself killed. Whatever happened to *do unto others?* In places like this, decent people didn't leave each other stranded in the cold.

His face was feeling stiff, and he figured he'd better start walking before his toes went numb. He struck out for a distant yard light, the only sign of human habitation in sight. He couldn't tell how distant, but he knew he'd be hurting by the time he got there, and he was counting on some kindly old man to be answering the door. No shame among the lame.

It wasn't like Zach was fresh off the operating table— it had been a few months since his last round of repairs— but he hadn't given himself enough time. He'd lopped a couple of weeks off the near end of the doc's estimated recovery time, rigged up a brace, done some heavy-duty taping and climbed onto another bull. Hung in there for five seconds—four seconds past feeling the pop in his hip and three seconds short of the buzzer.

He could still feel the pain shooting down his leg with every step. Only this time he had to pick the damn thing up, swing it forward and drop it down again on his own.

Pride be damned, he just hoped *somebody* would be answering the door at the end of the road. The light in the front window was a good sign.

The four steps to the covered porch might as well have

been four hundred, and he was looking to climb them with a lead weight chained to his left leg. His eyes were just as screwed up as his hip. Big black spots danced around with tiny red flashers, and he couldn't tell what was real and what wasn't. He stumbled over some shrubbery, steadied himself on the porch railing and peered between vertical slats.

There in the front window stood a spruce tree with a silver star affixed to the top. Zach was pretty sure the red sparks were all in his head, but the white lights twinkling by the hundreds throughout the huge tree, those were real. He wasn't too sure about the woman hanging the shiny balls. Most of her hair was caught up on her head and fastened in a curly clump, but the light captured by the escaped bits crowned her with a golden halo. Her face was a soft shadow, her body a willowy silhouette beneath a long white gown. If this was where the mind ran off to when cold started shutting down the rest of the body, then Zach's final worldly thought was, *This ain't such a bad way to go.*

If she would just turn to the window, he could die looking into the eyes of a Christmas angel.

* * * * *

Could this woman from Zach's past get the lonesome cowboy to come in from the cold...for good?
Look for
ONE COWBOY, ONE CHRISTMAS
by Kathleen Eagle
Available December 2009 from
Silhouette Special Edition®

Silhouette *Desire*

**FROM *NEW YORK TIMES*
BESTSELLING AUTHOR**

Diana
Palmer

THE
MAVERICK

A BRAND-NEW
LONG, TALL
TEXAN STORY

Visit Silhouette Books at www.eHarlequin.com

SD76982

HARLEQUIN® HISTORICAL:
Where love is timeless

**From chivalrous knights
to roguish rakes, look for the
variety Harlequin® Historical
has to offer every month.**

www.eHarlequin.com

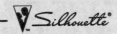
V *Silhouette®*

SPECIAL EDITION

**FROM *NEW YORK TIMES* AND *USA TODAY*
BESTSELLING AUTHOR**

KATHLEEN
EAGLE

ONE COWBOY,
One Christmas

When bull rider Zach Beaudry appeared
out of thin air on Ann Drexler's ranch,
she thought she was seeing a ghost of
Christmas past. And though Zach had
no memory of their night of passion years
ago, they were about to share a future
he would never forget.

*Available December 2009
wherever books are sold.*

Visit Silhouette Books at www.eHarlequin.com

REQUEST YOUR FREE BOOKS!
2 FREE NOVELS PLUS 2
FREE GIFTS!

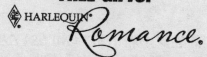

HARLEQUIN® *Romance*®

From the Heart, For the Heart

YES! Please send me 2 FREE Harlequin® Romance novels and my 2 FREE gifts (gifts are worth about $10). After receiving them, if I don't wish to receive any more books, I can return the shipping statement marked "cancel". If I don't cancel, I will receive 4 brand-new novels every month and be billed just $3.84 per book in the U.S. or $4.24 per book in Canada. That's a savings of at least 15% off the cover price! It's quite a bargain! Shipping and handling is just 50¢ per book.* I understand that accepting the 2 free books and gifts places me under no obligation to buy anything. I can always return a shipment and cancel at any time. Even if I never buy another book, the two free books and gifts are mine to keep forever.

114 HDN EYU3 314 HDN EYKG

Name	(PLEASE PRINT)	
Address		Apt. #
City	State/Prov.	Zip/Postal Code

Signature (if under 18, a parent or guardian must sign)

Mail to the **Harlequin Reader Service:**
IN U.S.A.: P.O. Box 1867, Buffalo, NY 14240-1867
IN CANADA: P.O. Box 609, Fort Erie, Ontario L2A 5X3

Not valid to current subscribers of Harlequin Romance books.

**Are you a subscriber of Harlequin Romance books
and want to receive the larger-print edition?
Call 1-800-873-8635 today!**

* Terms and prices subject to change without notice. Prices do not include applicable taxes. Sales tax applicable in N.Y. Canadian residents will be charged applicable provincial taxes and GST. Offer not valid in Quebec. This offer is limited to one order per household. All orders subject to approval. Credit or debit balances in a customer's account(s) may be offset by any other outstanding balance owed by or to the customer. Please allow 4 to 6 weeks for delivery. Offer available while quantities last.

Your Privacy: Harlequin Books is committed to protecting your privacy. Our Privacy Policy is available online at www.eHarlequin.com or upon request from the Reader Service. From time to time we make our lists of customers available to reputable third parties who may have a product or service of interest to you. If you would prefer we not share your name and address, please check here. ☐

HR09R

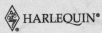

HARLEQUIN
Ambassadors

Want to share your passion for reading Harlequin® Books?

Become a Harlequin Ambassador!

Harlequin Ambassadors are a group of passionate and well-connected readers who are willing to share their joy of reading Harlequin® books with family and friends.

You'll be sent all the tools you need to spark great conversation, including free books!

All we ask is that you share the romance with your friends and family!

You'll also be invited to have a say in new book ideas and exchange opinions with women just like you!

To see if you qualify* to be a Harlequin Ambassador, please visit www.HarlequinAmbassadors.com.

*Please note that not everyone who applies to be a Harlequin Ambassador will qualify. For more information please visit www.HarlequinAmbassadors.com.

Thank you for your participation.

BAR09BPA